b

and a double-wide."

"What do you want, Mr. Tucker?" Dorian whispered. Better question, what was this man doing to her?

He looked at her intently. "I want smart, powerful people to respect me. It's the only way I can accomplish what I'm setting out to do. I know I have to earn their regard, and that's where you come in."

"Me?"

"Yep. I'm not worried about what's in here." He patted his chest with one hand. "Or here." He tapped his head. "But I need you to teach me how to act the part so people will believe in me."

The man was sincerity personified. There was nothing fake or phony or devious about him. Lord help her, Briny Tucker, the only millionaire in Slapdown, Texas, was the genuine article.

And she was charged with changing him.

Dear Reader,

Oh, baby! This June, Silhouette Romance has the perfect poolside reads for you, from babies to royalty, from sexy millionaires to rugged cowboys!

In Carol Grace's *Pregnant by the Boss!* (#1666), champagne and mistletoe lead to a night of passion between Claudia Madison and her handsome boss—but will it end in a lifetime of love? And don't miss the final installment in Marie Ferrarella's crossline miniseries, THE MOM SQUAD, with *Beauty and the Baby* (#1668), about widowed mother-to-be Lori O'Neill and the forbidden feelings she can't deny for her late husband's caring brother!

In Raye Morgan's *Betrothed to the Prince* (#1667), the second in the exciting CATCHING THE CROWN miniseries, a princess goes undercover when an abandoned baby is left in the care of a playboy prince. And some things are truly meant to be, as Carla Cassidy shows us in her incredibly tender SOULMATES series title, *A Gift from the Past* (#1669), about a couple given a surprising second chance at forever.

What happens when a rugged cowboy wins fifty million dollars? According to Debrah Morris, in *Tutoring Tucker* (#1670), he hires a sexy oil heiress to refine his rough-and-tumble ways, and they both get a lesson in love. Then two charity dating-game contestants get the shock of their lives when they discover *Oops...We're Married?* (#1671), by brand-new Silhouette Romance author Susan Lute.

See you next month for more fun-in-the-sun romances!

Happy reading!

Mary-Theresa Hussey

Mary-Theresa Hussey
Senior Editor

Please address questions and book requests to:
Silhouette Reader Service
U.S.: 3010 Walden Ave., P.O. Box 1325, Buffalo, NY 14269
Canadian: P.O. Box 609, Fort Erie, Ont. L2A 5X3

Tutoring Tucker

DEBRAH MORRIS

SILHOUETTE *Romance*®

Published by Silhouette Books

America's Publisher of Contemporary Romance

This book is dedicated to my sweet daughter,
because she restores my faith
in the world on a daily basis.

Caitlyn, I love you.
Don't ever stop believing in fairy tales.

 SILHOUETTE BOOKS

ISBN 0-373-19670-9

TUTORING TUCKER

Copyright © 2003 by Debrah Morris

This edition published by arrangement with Harlequin Books S.A.

® and TM are trademarks of Harlequin Books S.A., used under license.
Trademarks indicated with ® are registered in the United States Patent
and Trademark Office, the Canadian Trade Marks Office and in other
countries.

Visit Silhouette at www.eHarlequin.com

Printed in U.S.A.

Books by Debrah Morris

Silhouette Romance

A Girl, a Guy and a Lullaby #1549
That Maddening Man #1597
Tutoring Tucker #1670

DEBRAH MORRIS

Before embarking on a solo writing career, Debrah Morris coauthored over twenty romance novels as one half of the Pepper Adams/Joanna Jordan writing team. Married, and a mother of three, she loves wrtiting down her daydreams for others to read.

You can visit Debrah's Web site at ww.debrahmorris.com. If you wish to hear about upcoming releases, send an e-mail to: Debwilmor@aol.com or write to P.O. Box 522, Norman, OK 73070-0522. If you would like an auto-graphed bookmark, please send a SASE with your request.

All underlined places are fictitious.

Prologue

Sometimes fairy tales come true

Once upon a time in the dusty village of Slapdown in a western land called Texas, there lived a handsome, bighearted young pauper named Briny. He worked hard, but compassion made him poor. Quick to offer a helping hand to others, he often said, "What good is money, if it does not do good?"

Briny labored in the oil fields, toiling long hours to provide fuel for people across the land. Although he possessed little education, he was blessed with native intelligence and an abundance of generosity, purpose and honor. So much so that people called him a prince among men.

If fortune cookies indeed reveal truth, that success is truly measured in friends, then Briny considered himself a wealthy man.

He had, in fact, almost everything he wanted: the esteem of people who mattered, a small house on wheels, a loyal dog and a truck that ran most of the time. He needed but one thing to make his life complete—a fair maiden to love. A special lady to share his simple life and adore him above all others.

That was the wish Briny held close to his heart.

Ever optimistic, he knew it would someday come true, for he believed in the everlasting power of love. He did not worry about fate or destiny or other matters beyond his control, because he trusted in the notion that good things rewarded good deeds.

So Briny lived day to day, never planning ahead, and rarely concerned by what the future might bring. But because he was hopeful, he clung steadfastly to a single ritual. Each week he stopped by the Bag and Wag to buy a six-pack, a pizza and a ticket in the Great State Lottery.

He selected his six magic numbers carefully, choosing those imbued with special meaning. Twenty-nine because that was his age. Six for the number of boys who had shared his cottage at the juvenile home. Thirty-two for all the puppies Reba had delivered since being rescued from a cruel fate. Twenty for the number of letters in his name, Brindon Zachary Tucker. Eleven because that was how many years he had worked for Chaco Oil.

The last of his magical numbers was one.

For the one woman he would spend his life with.

Over time, Briny bought many tickets. He never won, yet he nurtured the hope that Lady Luck would yet smile upon him. Careful not to ask too much for himself, he wanted only enough to repay his debts, a truck that ran *all* the time and a little house *without* wheels on land he could call his own.

Briny made a vow, pledged before God and the Bag and Wag's aging proprietor. If by some miracle he should win, he would use his windfall treasure to make a difference in the world.

Cherishing his fanciful illusions, he slept soundly at night, little knowing his rare, simple life was about to change in ways he could not have imagined. For Briny, the generous young pauper who never dared to dream big, had no idea he was about to hit a jackpot beyond his wildest dreams.

But that was exactly what happened.

Chapter One

"I want to see Malcolm."

Maybe she wasn't having what her grandmother called a conniption fit, but Dorian Burrell had worked herself into a fine fizz during the nasty little scene at the bank. Normally she met with her financial manager over lunch at the country club. Driving through Dallas's frenetic lunch hour traffic to his high-rise office building had only enhanced her already impressive head of steam.

She breezed past the startled receptionist, in no mood to wait for the woman to acknowledge her. She had questions. She wanted answers. A big-haired girl in a knockoff DKNY blouse would not have them.

"Excuse me. I'm sorry. Miss Burrell?"

Dorian paused and deployed her most withering look. The one calculated to strike terror into the hearts of waiters, sales clerks and secretaries who dared to challenge her. "Yes?" Her tone was chilly enough to wilt the potted philodendron.

The young woman behind the desk flushed an unbecoming shade of red and ducked her fluffy head to scan an open appointment book. The poor girl really should see a professional about those split ends.

"I'm sorry, but I can't seem to find your name on the schedule. Is Mr. O'Neal expecting you?"

"Don't worry, he'll see me. *Tina.*" By emphasizing the receptionist's name, Dorian let her know she would be ill-advised to displease a kid-glove client.

"Wait. Please. I'll announce you." In a desperate attempt to carry out her duties, Tina reached for the intercom phone on her desk.

"Don't bother, I'll surprise him." This was a day for surprises. She'd had a few herself, none of which had been particularly pleasant. Dorian turned on three-inch heels and plowed through the heavy doors separating O'Neal's luxurious office from the richly paneled public area.

Malcolm was on the phone but smiled at his unannounced visitor and motioned her in. She'd like to see him stop her. He made excuses and wrapped up his conversation, as though eager to give his favorite client his undivided attention. "Why, Dorian, dear. To what do I owe this unexpected pleasure?"

"Cut the chitchat, Malcolm." She smoothed the short skirt of her ice-blue linen suit, folded her arms across her chest and perched on a corner of his massive teakwood desk. A long, silk-clad leg swung impatiently. "What the hell is going on?"

The man closed a folder, pushed his trendy little glasses up on his nose and frowned. "What do you mean?"

Malcolm O'Neal had a string of professional letters after his name and had handled the Burrell family's personal finances for years. He might be preternaturally astute about investments and stock portfolios, but his smooth, self-serving manner was mildly annoying.

"Okay, now you can cut what is known on the street as crap. I have a lunch date with Tiggy Moffatt at the Venetian Tea Room in—" she checked the diamond-encrusted watch on her wrist "—less than half an hour. I don't have time for games."

"You know I'd be happy to help you, Dorian, if I knew what the problem was." Malcolm frowned and brushed invisible lint from his lapel.

What a vain, dapper man. His tailored designer suit, fine

cotton shirt and carefully knotted silk tie had been purchased with the fees he charged her family. His dark hair was combed straight back, every thinning strand in place. He was clearly fiftysomething, yet there was no flash of silver there. He had to be coloring it.

"I'll tell you the problem," she said. "I stopped by the ATM to get some cash, and the machine ate my card."

"Really?" Despite efforts to sound concerned, Malcolm simply did not act sufficiently surprised.

"Yes, really." His underlying condescension grated on her already taut nerves, and she reined in the impulse to fling his Financial Planner of the Year paperweight across the room. "I figured the problem had to be a mistake or a glitch in the system, so I went inside."

"And?"

"The teller summoned a weasel-faced vice president who informed me my account is overdrawn. Can you believe that?"

Malcolm tapped his pursed lips with a long, elegant finger. "Well, you *have* been overdrawn before."

"I have not!"

"Perhaps you weren't aware of the problem because your grandmother arranged with the bank to cover overdrafts in the past."

She ignored the subtle yet pointed criticism. He was an employee, after all. If not hers, her grandmother's. "It's a couple of weeks until the next deposit from my trust fund, so I decided to get a cash advance on one of my credit cards. But weasel man confiscated them and would not give them back. Who does he think he is? I spent more money on shoes last year than he earned."

"Please sit down, Dorian." Malcolm waved her off his desk and into one of the straight-backed client chairs. "We need to talk."

"Yes, we do." She dropped into the chair, more confused now than angry. "Why would the banker do such a thing?"

"I'm afraid he was just following orders."

"Whose orders?"

"Pru's."

Dorian's eyes widened in disbelief. "My grandmother told some snotty little man to cut up my credit cards?"

"I'm afraid so." Malcolm leaned forward and steepled his fingers on the parchment blotter. "And it's not a 'couple of weeks' until the draft from your trust is deposited. It's *twelve* weeks."

"I've run out of money before. Granny Pru always covers my checks." She pulled an iridescent red cell phone from her tiny designer bag. "I'll just call her right now and get this mess straightened out."

Malcolm frowned. "I'm afraid you can't. She's out of the country."

"At the ranch?"

"She's not out *in* the country, dear. She's out *of* the country."

"As in…" Dorian prompted impatiently.

"At the moment she's on a Greek yacht in the Mediterranean, on the first leg of a rather long sea cruise. She instructed me to inform you she will be incommunicado for the next three months."

Stunned by the financial manager's bombshell, Dorian dropped the phone into her lap. "I don't understand."

"I believe your grandmother has cautioned you about your spending. Has she not urged you to live within your more than ample means?"

"Maybe. But she's always advanced me money before when I ran out."

Malcolm straightened his tie. "She said she warned you no more funds would be forthcoming if you were imprudent again."

Dorian glanced at the ceiling and sighed. True. Two weeks ago she'd been summoned to the North Park town house and reprimanded for what Granny Pru called "living too high on the hog." Having been dressed down before about her spending, she had scarcely listened. She'd been in a rush to meet her friends and make the opening of an exclusive new West End club.

"So what are you telling me, Malcolm?"

"You want the nutshell version?"

"Please. I've already had the lecture, parts one, two and three."

"Simply put, you are out of money." At her disbelieving look, he elaborated. "Strapped. Flat broke. Busted. The industry term for your current condition is insolvent."

She laughed, relieving the tension that had built inside her. If she didn't laugh, she might cry. And Dorian Burrell did not cry in public. She saved her tears for the lonely darkness. "You're kidding, right?"

Malcolm's brows lifted, reminding her he rarely dabbled in kidding.

Broke? She slumped in the chair. Having known nothing but wealth and privilege, she could scarcely conceive of the concept. Icy fear snaked through her. She was broke. "So what am I supposed to do now?"

"That's what we have to figure out," Malcolm said gently.

Her thoughts raced to make sense of an impossible, improbable situation. Would she be forced from the apartment her grandmother had given her when she graduated college? Part of a luxury West End renovation project, the penthouse commanded a fantastic view of the city and was close to the trendiest restaurants and night spots. Maybe she didn't hold the deed or pay the bills, but she had personally chosen every item in her home, the only place she felt secure.

The houses she'd grown up in had never been homes. They'd been cold and empty, decorated by professionals, managed by housekeepers and cleaned by maids in gray uniforms. Her mother had floated through the artfully arranged rooms like an amorphous spirit, beautiful and not quite real.

Always untouchable.

"What about my apartment?" Dorian voiced her concern.

"Pru was explicit. You're to continue living there."

Relieved, she blinked back another sting of tears. This time they were tears of gratitude—even rarer for her than those of sadness or self-pity.

"But I have no money?" She would have figured her

chances of uttering that particular combination of words in her lifetime were considerably less than, 'I'm catching the red-eye to Mars.''

"Not until your next trust deposit."

"Which is in September.

"Right."

"This is June."

Malcolm consulted his fancy desk calendar. "Correct."

"I don't believe this. What am I supposed to do until then? Did Granny Pru leave any words of wisdom before going incommunicado?"

"She said she was confident you could solve this problem on your own. You do come from strong stock, you know."

"Please, spare me the salt-of-the-earth story. I know all about how great-grandfather Portis started out with nothing but a hundred dollars and a wildcatter's dream. How he pulled himself up by his bootstraps to build one of the biggest, richest oil companies in Texas." She pushed out of the chair and paced in front of the desk, her blond bob swinging.

As heir to the Chaco Oil fortune, currently controlled by her seventy-nine-year-old grandmother, she was well acquainted with family propaganda. "What the hell are bootstraps anyway?"

He shuffled papers in an attempt to hide his smile.

"I'm glad you think this is funny, Malcolm. Because I don't."

"I think your grandmother hoped you would look at the next ninety days as a learning experience."

"Right." Uncertainty coursed through Dorian, an unfamiliar emotion for someone who'd always been sure of her place in the world. Now that world was threatened. How could she manage without her grandmother's love and support? Her father was dead. Her mother barely deserved the title. Granny Pru was the only person she could depend on. "Does she hate me?"

"You know better," Malcolm said. "She loves you. Always has."

"Is she trying to punish me?" Other than being born into

the right family, Dorian had done nothing to deserve the advantages handed her on an heirloom silver platter. She had always stuffed the feelings of unworthiness down in the place where she stored all unacceptable emotions.

"I'm sure that's not the case."

"Oh, my God." She stopped pacing and whirled to face him. "Has Granny Pru gone senile? Please tell me she hasn't lost her mind."

"No, of course not." Malcolm dismissed the idea as absurd. "Prudence Channing Burrell is the sharpest, most savvy and sensible woman I know."

"Then I give up. Did she mention why she feels compelled to turn her only grandchild's life into a waking nightmare?"

"Actually, she said if you asked, I was to give you a one-word answer."

"Which would be?"

"Cassandra." He leaned back in his chair, apparently pleased with his cryptic response.

What did her self-absorbed mother have to do with anything? Pru and Cassandra had engaged in a bitter mother-in-law versus daughter-in-law battle for over two decades. Since John Burrell's death thirteen years ago, his merry widow had maintained a palatial home in Dallas, but spent most of the year jetting around the country with her snooty, old-money friends. The last Dorian heard she was summering at Hyannis Port, still trying to worm her way into the Kennedy enclave.

Cassandra Burrell hired out unpleasant tasks. She had gardeners to clip hedges, chauffeurs to drive cars, cooks to prepare food and maids to clean up. She would have rented a womb if she hadn't accidentally gotten pregnant first. Since she found motherhood an especially odious chore, she'd brought in a succession of nannies to perform the duties she found distasteful.

Early on, Dorian had learned to torment and manipulate the poor women paid to care for her. All in the foolish hope that if she could drive them away Cassandra would become a sweet, loving mother who gave hugs and kisses and cuddles. Dorian's childhood tantrums were legend. If she wanted a bed-

time story, she ordered the nanny to read. If she wanted a
cookie at five in the morning, she sent the nanny to fetch one.
If she flung her expensive clothes from drawers and closets,
she waited for the nanny to put them away.

The one thing Dorian had not been able to order was the
thing she had longed for most of all. Her mother's love. She'd
given up that dream years ago. "Since when has my mother
helped anyone? Especially me."

"I don't think Pru meant for you to seek Cassandra's assistance, Dorian. I believe your mother is meant to be an object
lesson for you."

"A what?"

"Think about it."

She was thinking, but not about her narcissistic, emotionally
distant mother. "Wait. I know! I'll liquefy something."

"I assume you mean liquidate."

Dorian waved her hand. "Whatever. I'll sell the Mercedes
and buy something cheaper, like a Lexus."

"I don't think the leasing company would approve of you
disposing of their property."

"Oh. Right." She flipped a strand of chin-length hair behind her ear. "Tell me again why I lease?"

"Because you like to drive a new vehicle every few
months."

She knew there had to be a reason. "Then I'll just take out
a loan that I can repay in September."

"Maybe I didn't make myself clear." Malcolm leaned forward. "Your grandmother has pulled the plug, so to speak, on
your finances. All your credit cards have been suspended, including your retail charge accounts. Even if you qualified for
a loan, which you don't since you have no credit history, you
could not get one."

"Why not? I'm a responsible adult." Legally, at twenty-six
she was an adult. But responsible? Dorian tried to recall the
name of a girl she'd met in college. She'd worn discount-
center clothes and ridden a rusty old bike, but she'd had goals.
Purpose. She'd been a responsible adult at seventeen.

Mallory Peterson. Dorian hadn't thought about the quiet,

mousy honor student in years. They'd only spoken once, in the library, when Dorian had asked for help locating a book.

The girl had seemed eager to cultivate Dorian's interest. Her mother waited tables, her father drove a truck. And yet she wanted to be a doctor, the first in her nowhere, west Texas town. Every month she received a small stipend, donated by townspeople, so she could stay in school and realize her dream. When she earned her medical degree she planned to return to take care of them.

Having earned a full scholarship, Mallory had received her good-faith money because people believed in her. Dorian, on the other hand, had done nothing to deserve the generous allowance her family deemed her due. She was in school because of her grandmother's influence.

The earnest premed student had made Dorian feel so ashamed she had retreated to her shallow sorority sisters, spurning what might have become a real friendship with a person who could have taught her something about responsibility. Regret weighed like a stone on her mind as she refocused on what Malcolm was saying.

"I think you can forget about a loan, dear. Prudence Burrell's influence is far-reaching. There's not a lending institution, pawnshop or loan shark named Guido in the Dallas-Fort Worth area who'd risk giving you a nickel now."

"She can do that?" Dorian knew her grandmother was powerful, but hadn't realized just how powerful until now. She sank back in the chair, unable to decide if she was frustrated, angry or simply terrified of what the next ninety days would bring. Then there was the regret thing. And the awful suspicion that without money Dorian Burrell did not amount to much.

"She already has. There *is* something you can do," he suggested tentatively.

"What? Jump off a bridge?"

"You could get a job."

She laughed. "What in God's name could I do?"

"I'm sure you could find something. You're a college graduate."

"From a school whose art history department is housed in Burrell Hall, and whose scholarship program is endowed by my grandmother. The dean was grateful enough to overlook things like grades."

"Still, you must have learned something in four years."

"I majored in art history," she reminded him. "Which really only qualifies me to visit museums. I minored in classical mythology. Seen any openings for a CEO of myths lately?"

Dammit. How had she let this happen? She was smart. She had money. Why hadn't she done something with her life? While shopping, lunching and partying filled time, they did not fulfill much purpose.

She hadn't always been without goals. Once in seventh grade one of her boarding school instructors told her the poetry she'd written had merit. One night at a rare dinner with her mother, she had announced her desire to be a teacher. Shaping young minds had seemed like a worthy vocation.

Cassandra had laughed.

"There are always entry-level jobs," Malcolm pointed out.

The idea filled Dorian with the same curiosity and disgust she'd felt while dissecting fetal pigs in high school biology. "I don't think so." She'd been far too hard on waitresses, clerks and receptionists over the years to try and join their ranks now.

"Face the facts, Malcolm. I have no marketable skills. No experience. I don't even have a résumé. If I did, I'd have to list debutante as my former occupation." Why had she never realized before today that she was practically useless to society?

Malcolm glanced at his gold Rolex. "I'm sorry to cut this short, but I have a new client due. You have a lot to absorb, Dorian. Go to lunch with your friend. Think about what we've discussed and call me later."

"I will." She dropped her phone back into her bag and rose as the receptionist buzzed to announce Malcolm's next appointment. She paused at the door. "I can't do lunch. I have no credit cards or cash." The words felt as strange and distasteful in her mouth as a jalapeño lollipop.

Malcolm pulled out his wallet and extracted four crisp twenties. "I'm not supposed to do this. Pru would have my head if she knew, but I think you need to meet your friend as planned." He handed her the money. "It's not much, but should cover lunch."

"Thanks." Dorian tucked the bills into her bag. Never had she felt so grateful for so little. What would eighty dollars buy? A few meals. A couple of tanks of gas. A massage. A manicure. A small jar of her favorite moisturizer. Not all of those things. One. She'd never had to make hard choices before.

Stepping into the outer office, she eyed the rough-looking man perched uncomfortably on a chair in reception. He rose when she entered, as though someone who had taught him good manners dictated he do so. He grinned, and his long-lashed blue eyes crinkled at the corners.

He obviously liked what he saw, but Dorian was accustomed to that reaction from men. She gave him her patented "in your dreams" look, expecting him to turn away.

He didn't flinch. He stood on Malcolm's silver-gray carpet with his hands clasped behind his back and looked her right in the eye. He forced *her* to avert her glance. The nerve! This Neanderthal couldn't be the new client. He wouldn't know what a financial manager did, much less require the services of one. He had laborer written all over him and couldn't have gotten past security unless he was here to change the air-conditioning filters or unclog the toilet. Clearly blue-collar, he looked as out of place in the plush office as a frog in a punch bowl.

But not nearly as nervous.

Tall and sinewy, he sported the kind of muscles a man got by working hard, not from working out. And chances were he hadn't paid to have his skin bronzed. His tan had the natural look of one acquired the old-fashioned way, by spending a lot of time outdoors, far from a tennis court or swimming pool. He exuded a hard-core masculinity so raw and elemental Dorian could almost hear him sweat.

She was inexplicably drawn to his blatant virility, then

shocked by the gut-punch power of her response. Ridiculous!
She needed some serious aromatherapy to clear her head. Raw
and elemental was not her style. No way could she be attracted
to anyone so…inappropriate.

The object of her short-circuited desire was dressed in a
stiff pair of jeans that hugged his narrow hips, long legs and
taut rear. His blue shirt still bore creases from the packaging,
the sleeves rolled back on his brawny forearms. His drooping
Magnum P.I. mustache was straight out of the seventies and
his dark hair was cut like Mel Gibson in *Lethal Weapon*, dis-
tinctive but passé. At least his 'do was a decade less dated
than his facial hair.

Dorian glanced down as she passed. Shoes revealed a lot
about a man, and his were brand-new, pointy-toed cowboy
boots. Figured. She favored Italian loafers herself, and the kind
of men who wore them, but she caught Tina ogling Mr. Pher-
omone appreciatively as she ushered him into Malcolm's office. Yeah, he was definitely the type who'd make the receptionist's heart go pitty-pat. All hormones and hair.

New boots and no future.

By the time she arrived at the Venetian Tea Room and
kissed the air beside Tiggy Moffatt's cheek, Dorian had already forgotten Malcolm's caveman cowboy. For the first time
in her life she had real problems.

Best friends since grade school, Tiggy sized up Dorian's
mood with the experience of many years of shared confi-
dences. "Who spit in your wheat grass protein shake this
morning?"

"I have had the most incredibly horrible day." She accepted a menu from the eager waiter, who was already flirting
to increase his tip. She was not in the mood. "And it's only
noon."

"What happened?" Tiggy folded her arms on the table.

They ordered, and Dorian relayed the story while they
waited for their food. She even included the part where she
had to accept Malcolm O'Neal's paltry wad of twenties. A
minor humiliation really, compared to the major disaster her
life had become. Tiggy was sympathetic but on a tight allow-

ance herself. Her trust fund was a mere shadow of Dorian's, and since she wasn't exactly the creative type, Tiggy had little to offer in the way of suggestions.

"Is there a problem with the Cobb salad, miss?" The waiter hovered at Dorian's elbow.

Yes, there was a problem. She hadn't wanted a salad. Compelled to scan the right side of the menu, she'd chosen the least expensive item listed. Then she'd lost her appetite when she realized for the first time that many people probably couldn't afford *anything* on *any* menu. She'd had a disconcerting flashback to the night she and her friends had cut through an alley and seen a dirty man digging through the restaurant's trash cans. They'd shuddered, joked and gone on their irresponsible way. Why hadn't they given the poor soul some money?

They'd had more than enough.

"I'm just not hungry." She pushed the plate of salad a few inches away. "Bring me another glass of wine, please." If she had more cash, she'd order the bottle. Normally, she didn't try to drown her troubles, but a little judicious soaking wouldn't hurt.

"Do you want a to-go carton, miss?"

"Of course not." How gauche to wag leftovers home from a restaurant. Then she thought of the empty shelves in her imported French cabinets. There wasn't much in her restaurant-size chrome refrigerator, either, and she wasn't about to spend any of her precious dollars on groceries. She smiled up at the waiter. "On second thought, why don't you box that salad up for me, sweetie?"

"What are you going to do?" Tiggy asked after the waiter returned with the wine and removed the neglected salad.

"Eat leftover Cobb salad for dinner, I guess."

"No, what are you going to do for money, hon?"

"I don't know. Care to buy some jewelry?"

"I wish. But I can't." Tiggy glossed her lips with a tiny wand. "I'm living pretty close to the edge myself these days."

"What *am* I going to do?"

Tiggy shrugged. "I heard one of mother's maids say she

lives on oriental noodles when she runs out of money before payday. You could probably buy a whole case of those for eighty dollars."

"Maybe I'll hole up in my apartment until this nightmare is over."

"Yuck. How fun is that? Oh, no! Does this mean you won't be flying to Cozumel with us after all?"

Dorian groaned. A large group of her favorite friends were planning a week at a resort on the exotic Mexican isle. This time yesterday, she'd assumed she would be sipping frozen margaritas on the beach alongside them. Now that seemed unlikely. She had never questioned their loyalty, but how would they react to her current state of forced insolvency? If their acceptance was based on her net worth, might they dismiss her as easily as they had the hungry man at the trash can?

She longed for Tiggy's reassurance but didn't dare share her misgivings with anyone, not even her best friend. Better to keep doubts hidden. They would grow in the light of day and eat away what was left of her shriveled self-confidence, like so many insect-devouring plants.

"Are you kidding?" Maybe derision would hide her insecurity. "I couldn't finance a trip to a mud bank on the Brazos at the moment."

The tinny strains of "The Eyes of Texas are Upon You" jangled from Dorian's bag. She checked her phone, and Malcolm's private office number appeared on caller ID. "What?" she asked without preamble. "Did Granny Pru discover your duplicity and demand you take your eighty bucks back?"

She leaned against the banquette and listened. Her financial manager swore he had the answer to her unprayed prayers. When he finished, she said, "Now I know you're kidding. Oh, wait. I forgot. You don't have a sense of humor. Which means you think I would seriously consider such a ridiculous suggestion."

Malcolm refused to take no for an answer and threw in a crack about her temporarily desperate circumstances. He made her promise to return to his office immediately. Short on options, Dorian reluctantly agreed and placed the phone back in her purse. "I have to go." She stood, picked up the plastic box of salad the waiter had placed on the table and fished in her purse for one of the precious twenties.

Tiggy tossed back her long, dark hair and placed a couple of bills in the check folder. "Let me get this. Save your money. You might need it."

"Thanks." She'd often picked up the tab for Tiggy and others in her circle. So why did she feel strange accepting her friend's gesture? Did those who had to accept charity feel even worse? A guest at many fund-raising galas, she hadn't once considered the recipients of those funds.

"What was that all about?" Tiggy asked. "Good news I hope."

"Depends on your definition of good." The two women model-walked through the dining room, turning male heads as they passed. "Are you ready for this? Malcolm claims he found me a job."

"Already? Good Lord! Doing what?"

"Apparently some redneck I saw in his office today just won the lottery, and he wants someone to teach him how to be a man of culture. Kind of like Henry Higgins and Eliza Doolittle. Only reversed." At Tiggy's blank look, she added, "*My Fair Lady*? The movie? Rex Harrison and Audrey Hepburn?"

"Oh, yeah. And he's willing to pay you to tutor him?"

"Apparently so. He wants someone to take him from roughshod to refined. To help him buy the right clothes, choose the right home, teach him to appreciate fine wine and gourmet food. According to Malcolm, he wants to learn to dance at balls and understand art and literature."

"That sounds like your kind of job."

"No, what it sounds like is a job for a freaking fairy godmother. Too bad I'm fresh out of magic wands."

Stepping out of the cool restaurant into the bright midday sun, they crossed the parking lot and stopped to talk beside Tiggy's Porsche.

"Malcolm says the man wants to be a *real* gentleman, so he can move with confidence in civilized circles. Apparently, he wants to understand how the millionaire mind works and use his nouveau riches for the good of his fellow man.''

"How noble," said Tiggy sarcastically. "He's a regular philanderer.''

"Philanthropist," Dorian corrected absently. She was still trying to understand what kind of perverse fate made a poor man rich and a rich woman poor. Life simply wasn't fair.

"So, do you think you'll take the job?''

"I don't know.''

"You should," Tiggy urged. "Sounds like fun.''

"Fun would not be my primary motivation. Fairy godmother or not, I guess if an incredibly lucky bumpkin needs someone to spend his money and teach him the difference between a shrimp fork and a demitasse spoon, Dorian Channing Burrell is his woman.''

"You go, girl!'' Tiggy used her keyless entry device to unlock the car door and ducked inside. "By the way, how much did he win?''

Dorian sighed. That was the biggest irony of all. "Fifty million dollars.''

Chapter Two

Briny Tucker glanced up from the magazine he was too nervous to read. The financial planner's receptionist was staring at him. Again. She smiled, and he smiled back in what he hoped was a friendly yet discouraging manner. He didn't want to hurt the poor girl's feelings, but all the calf-eyed looks she kept shooting his way made him as jumpy as a tick on a hot rock.

He rubbed his sweaty palms on his jeans and eyed the door to Malcolm O'Neal's inner office. What was taking so long? His errant gaze tangled with the receptionist's again, and they danced through the smiley face routine one more time. Behaving like a gentleman could be a nuisance. He had accepted the coffee she offered when he didn't want any, and he had tried to make small talk when he didn't know how. He had even slipped the piece of paper containing her home phone number into his pocket, knowing he'd never give her a call.

Yeah, he sure enough needed lessons in how to be a gentleman.

He stroked his mustache and snapped his gum, two nervous habits he couldn't seem to break. Normally he would be flattered by a pretty girl coming on to him, but wide-eyed, fluffy-

haired Tina with her silky outfit and shiny nails was obviously
out of his league. He was accustomed to dating girls who
dressed up in rhinestone-studded T-shirts. Tina probably went
out with men who wore ties every day and knew why a guy
needed more than one fork. For the first time in his life he
wondered if her interest was in him or his money.

Money? As in *Who Wants To Be a Millionaire*. Whoa! Hard
to believe, but Briny Tucker really was one. About fifty times
over. He still had trouble wrapping his mind around that amazing fact. Practicing the words in front of the hotel mirror last
night had paid off—he could finally string them together in
his thoughts without laughing out loud. Or looking around to
see who else, besides God, was in on the joke.

Recent events did not seem real. Briny Tucker a millionaire.
And all because he'd lucked out and finally picked the right
string of numbers. Even after Uncle Sam's sizable cut, he had
more cash than any man had a right to bank in one lifetime.

But being rich wasn't all fun and games. That's why he'd
asked around until he'd learned who handled his employer's
money. Anyone good enough for Prudence Burrell was good
enough for him. The burden to do something meaningful with
his windfall was a heavy weight that burned his gut and
twisted his heart until getting out from under the responsibility
was all he could think about. That's why he was here. Trying
to do the smart thing. He had a lot to learn before he could
live up to the responsibility that had been heaped on his shoulders.

Careful not to let his gaze tangle with Tina's, he angled a
quick peek at the door leading to O'Neal's office. His classy
would-be tutor had disappeared through there when she bar-
reled by a while ago. The financial planner said he needed a
few minutes alone with Miss Burrell to explain the position
Briny had to offer. What was taking so long? He checked his
watch, the case scratched and battered from working on the
oil rigs. Half an hour. Explaining must have turned into convincing. Or arm twisting.

Maybe he was wasting his time. The fact that Dorian Burrell
was heir to the very company that Briny had worked for, up

until a week ago, had seemed like another lucky coincidence when O'Neal first mentioned what he had in mind. Now that he'd had a second look at the pampered petroleum princess, he wasn't sure she was the best hand for the job. Oh, the cool, blond, trust-fund baby could teach him what he needed to know in order to run with society's big dogs—Dorian Burrell had flounced into the world with a sterling silver spoon clamped firmly between her perfect, pearly white teeth—that was not the problem.

Unlike the moony young receptionist, the hoity-toity oil heiress had looked at him down that pretty nose of hers as if he was something she'd stepped in while crossing the corral.

Briny didn't know much about the world beyond the oil fields, but he was pretty sure flat-out scorn wouldn't help him achieve his goals. The tutoring process was meant to *increase* his confidence, not blast it into fifty million pieces.

"If you have a better idea, Dorian, please share." Malcolm O'Neal leaned back in his ergonomically engineered leather desk chair and adjusted his glasses. "This job didn't fall into your lap out of pure dumb luck, you know. It's definitely a miracle. I should probably notify the Vatican."

"Very funny," she muttered. Her overwrought fingers drummed a steady tattoo on the arm of her chair. Just because she'd had time to adjust to the fact of her impoverishment, didn't mean she had to like the idea. "I'm glad you find my misfortune so amusing."

"Dorian, as your financial manager, I highly recommend you take the job. I rather doubt you'll find anyone in the universe willing to pay one-tenth of what my client has offered for your services, or any job better suited to your particular, ah, talents."

"Thanks for the vote of confidence, Malcolm." Dorian knew he was right. She just hated that he was. Thirty thousand dollars was a lot of money for three months' work. What was she worried about? She could handle this. Malcolm said she wouldn't have to teach the nouveau riche Neanderthal everything. She could concentrate on appearance, etiquette, culture and the finer points of social grace while coordinating the numerous instructors, classes and training courses Briny Tucker would need to bring him up to millionaire-socialite speed.

Briny. What kind of name was that?

"As chief miracle worker, I get to call the shots, right? Run the show? Be the boss?" Otherwise she wanted nothing to do with this real-life Technicolor episode of the *Beverly Hillbillies*.

"Of course. Mr. Tucker has agreed to defer to your judgment in all things pertaining to his, ah, grooming."

"Do I have to sign anything?"

"Just a standard business contract outlining your duties and terms of the agreement. Nothing to worry about." He dismissed her concern with a hand flap and avoided making eye contact as he pushed a piece of legal-size paper across the desk. "I took the liberty of having this drawn up before you arrived."

"Pretty darned sure of yourself, weren't you?"

"Like I said, if you have a better idea…"

"I don't know." Signing a contract was a bigger commitment than Dorian had ever made before. A contract sounded official, binding. Scary.

"Three months isn't such a long time." Malcolm clearly wanted to close the deal, but Dorian refused to be rushed.

"Maybe not to someone with money coming in," she snapped. The eighty dollars in her purse wouldn't last through tomorrow afternoon. And if Malcolm thought she'd give the money back because he'd found her a job, he was in for a surprise. She glanced at the contract to confirm the figure he'd quoted her. "This Tucker person is really willing to pay that amount?"

"It's all spelled out in black-and-white." Malcolm slid a fancy platinum pen toward her. "Just sign, and we can move on."

She was sorely tempted. As an ex-debutante with no employment history, minimal prospects, and if truth be told, no marketable skills whatsoever, she knew exactly how miraculous the offer was. Almost too good to be true. A ready solution to an unexpected cash flow problem. And far more palatable than bagging burgers at a fast-food counter.

She would definitely not look her best in a cardboard hat.

"What's more, he's willing to pay one month's wages in advance." This time Malcolm slid a check across the desk. "As his financial manager, I've been authorized to offer you the first payment today."

"Oh, you have, have you?" This out-of-the-blue, too-easy solution smelled like a trap. She should kick off her new Ferragamo pumps and sprint to the nearest exit before she did something stupid. She had to be crazy. Why else would she even consider spending the next few months in forced proximity to a totally unsuitable man with whom she had nothing in common? One whose physical presence had made her aware of his inappropriateness in the most alarming way both times she'd passed him in Malcolm's waiting room.

"He is an altogether intriguing, ingenuous young man," Malcolm went on. "You'll like him, if you give him half a chance. And I think Pru will agree, this may be a growth experience for you as well as him. She'll be pleased you solved your problem and impressed by your resourcefulness."

Anything to get back into Granny Pru's good graces. "Oh, all right. I'll sign." Without bothering to read the fine print, Dorian grabbed the contract and scribbled her name across the bottom before she changed her mind. She tucked the check into her purse before Malcolm changed his. Growth experience or not, she was not sure she could ever forgive her grandmother for thrusting her into this horrible position.

Malcolm rubbed his hands together in satisfaction and rocked forward in his chair. "Excellent." He punched the desk intercom. "Tina, please show Mr. Tucker in."

Dorian groaned. "And please show me where you keep the Valium."

Five minutes of Mr. Tucker's company told Dorian ninety days would not be nearly enough time to buck Darwin's theory and polish the hairy missing link into something remotely resembling a socialite. She had expected him to be rough around the edges. She was wrong. Tucker was a gum-chewing, hobnailed yokel of staggering proportions, who readily admitted he studied "rich folks" by watching *Dallas* reruns on satellite television. Raw and unpolished to the core. An unlikely, mustachioed blip on Lady Luck's radar.

Dorian assessed the new millionaire. "Given time constraints and the current state of technology, complete molecular reconstruction is out. So to achieve positive results, the transformation process will have to be intense."

"Whatever you say, ma'am. Like I told Mr. O'Neal, you're the boss."

For maximum effect, and for her own convenience, which she prized above all things, Dorian suggested her student move out of the hotel where he currently resided and into her West End apartment. "If not for the duration, at least until I can help you find a suitable place to live."

"I don't know about that, ma'am." Tucker's baritone was marred by a west Texas drawl. "Doesn't seem quite right. Me living with you and all. I'd hate to get underfoot."

His polite demurral possessed a certain Jed Clampett-esque charm, but a dialect coach would rid his speech of its twangy nuances soon enough. One of the first things Dorian had learned in her snooty Connecticut boarding school was the inverse relationship between regional dialect and perceived IQ. The stronger the accent, the less intelligent people thought you were.

"Don't be foolish," she told him. "We need a base of operations for your studies, and I prefer to have you close at hand. I can't promise results if you're not fully immersed in your new lifestyle, 24/7."

"But—"

"My apartment is quite large, and I have three extra bedrooms. You will hardly be underfoot, I assure you."

"Well." She winced as he drew the word out into two syllables. "I see your point, ma'am, but sharing living quarters doesn't seem quite proper."

"If you're worried about impropriety, don't trouble yourself. I promise not to compromise you in any way." Surely

her frosty tone let him know she would not touch him if provided with a ready supply of ten-foot poles.

"Oh, I'm not worried about that, ma'am." His grin
morphed into an embarrassed grimace. "I was thinking about
your reputation."

Her reputation? How gallant and provincial. Who considered such things these days?

Tucker gave Dorian a long, assessing look, his bristly brows
bunched in indecision. Malcolm gave him an encouraging nod,
and he said, "I suppose if Mr. O'Neal thinks it's all right."

"I'll vouch for Ms. Burrell's sincerity when she says you
have nothing to fear in that area," Malcolm said solemnly.

Tucker shrugged. "Okay, then. I guess I'll move in with
you. Truth is, it's kind of a relief. Hotel living's getting expensive, and Reba really hates staying there."

"Reba?" Dorian blinked, startled by the unexpected revelation. Malcolm failed to mention the bumpkin had brought a
bumpkiness along for the ride. "Your wife?"

"My dog. We've been together so long, I couldn't bear to
leave her behind in Slapdown. She would've pined away."

"I see. How touching." He must have greased quite a few
palms to keep an animal at the Fairmont. She couldn't decide
which was more confusing. His loyalty to his dog or his will-
ingness to pay to keep the mutt near. Maybe there was more
to the man than met the eye.

What was she thinking? Of course there was more to him.
Fifty million dollars more.

With Malcolm overseeing, they concluded their arrange-
ments. Dorian gave Tucker her address, and he promised to
present himself promptly at ten o'clock the following morning
to begin the makeover process. They stood, and she extended
her hand to close the deal. The suddenly rich former oil rig
foreman engulfed her small, manicured hand in both of his,
infusing her skin with electrifying warmth as he pumped up
and down.

"I sure thank you for taking me on like this, Miss Burrell.
I need all the help I can get, and with a lady like you, well, I
know I'll learn from the best."

"I'll certainly try to be of assistance to you, Mr. Tucker."
Dorian wanted to break the connection between them, to re-
claim both her hand and her sense of control, yet couldn't
summon the strength. She was trapped, pinned in the vivid
blue headlights of Briny Tucker's long-lashed eyes. Eyes that
looked deep into her and reflected more than she knew was
there.

"See," he continued, oblivious to his startling effect on her,
"I won this money for a reason. Well, I didn't really *win*
anything. I was singled out for a gift from above and I'm
supposed to do something meaningful with what I've been
given."

"Is that so?"

"Why, sure. What good is money, if money doesn't do
good?"

Was this guy for real? He was either the biggest fraud or
the most chillingly earnest man she had ever encountered.
"Who said that?" She didn't recognize the quotation.

"I did. I made a promise, if I ever hit the jackpot, I'd use
the money to make a difference in the world. See what I'm
saying?"

"Who did you promise?" Her words were necessarily
breathy, since the unprecedented drop in oxygen level. What
was sucking all the air out of the room?

He grinned, and another wave of unidentified emotion
washed over her. He had the sweetest, purest smile Dorian had
ever seen on anyone not officially a member of the seraphim
or cherubim.

"Why, I promised me." Tucker's eyes turned heavenward.
"And Him."

"And you believe a promise is a promise." Dorian wasn't
sure she'd ever met anyone who shared that ideal. In her experience promises were easily made and easily broken, when
keeping them became difficult or inconvenient. How long had
she clung to her mother's many promises before realizing they
were nothing but empty words?

"Well, sure." He exhaled, as though deeply relieved. "Boy

howdy, I'm glad you understand where I'm coming from, Miss Burrell.''

But did she? Tucker clearly kept his promises. She had the unwelcome thought that any woman on the receiving end of so much sincerity would be lucky indeed. That confused her more than ever. Could the man she'd written off as a simpleton actually have layers? ''I'm not sure I do understand.'' He squeezed her hand. Longing to feel that rare tingling warmth more intensely, she fought the shocking urge to fall into his arms.

''I don't want to be just another blustering redneck in hand-tooled boots, with a big truck and a double-wide.'' His voice was slow, deep, hypnotic. ''Why, a man like that is no more than a clown. Smart, powerful people would take advantage of him. He doesn't deserve a gift.''

''What do you want, Mr. Tucker?'' she whispered. Better question, what was he doing to her?

He looked at her intently, his gentle expression melting some of the ice inside her until she questioned her sanity again. ''I want smart, powerful people to respect me. It's the only way I can accomplish what I'm setting out to do. I know I have to earn their regard, and that's where you come in.''

''Me?'' The sound was more gulp than word.

''Yep. I'm not worried about what's in here.'' He patted his chest with one hand while clutching hers with the other. ''Or here.'' He tapped his head.

''I know what I have to do. But I need you to teach me how to act the part so people will believe in me.''

''That's an admirable ambition.'' And one heck of an assignment. Dorian slipped her hand free and gradually regained the power of thought she had lost when Tucker touched her. What was the matter with her? She didn't do warm and tingly. Something was very wrong here. She would have to keep a tighter rein on all her body parts when this guy was around.

She crossed the room and opened the door, hoping he would take the hint and leave so she could pull herself together. ''I'll see you tomorrow, then.''

"Oh, I'll be there, Miss Burrell, ma'am." He gave her a quick wink. "With bells on."

Then he smiled again, and the heat slipped past her reserve to warm the cold corners of her heart. What had Malcolm called the man? Intriguing and ingenuous. Yes, he was those things. He was something else, too, something she was unfamiliar with and couldn't quite name.

Not until his lanky form disappeared through the door and down the hall did she realize what set him apart from every other man she'd ever met.

The man was sincerity personified. There was nothing fake or phony or devious about him. She closed Malcolm's office door and leaned against it. Lord help her. Briny Tucker, the only millionaire in Slapdown, Texas, was the genuine article.

And she was charged with changing him.

The doorbell rang as Dorian stepped out of the shower. Great. Leave it to Slapdown to be on time. She wrapped a thick towel around her wet hair and pulled on a short satin robe, which she cinched at the waist.

"First lesson of the day," she admonished as she yanked open the door. "Never show up at the agreed-upon time. It's extremely bad form."

"Oh, yeah?"

Her gaze took in his grinning face, then dropped lower to settle on a most disturbing sight. "Omigod!"

"What's wrong?" Tucker was startled by her one-word assessment of the companion panting at his side.

"You said you had a dog." She looked accusingly at the quivering mass of flopping ears, drooping jowls and bloodshot eyes. "Is that supposed to be a dog?"

"Yes, ma'am." He swept off his cowboy hat and tried valiantly not to acknowledge her state of undress. His awkward gaze swept down to her bare feet, up her legs, over her chest and back up to the towel on her head.

His efforts at not noticing made Dorian more aware of her nakedness beneath the thin layer of sapphire satin. She clutched the lapels of her robe together. "Are you sure?"

Gentleman that he was, he did not allow his eyes to wander. "Miss Burrell, meet Reba. She's just about the sweetest old bloodhound in Texas. She was the best tracker in the county until she lost her nose."

Dorian eyed the so-called dog and the damp slime trail of saliva on the foyer's one-hundred-dollar-a-yard carpet. "That beast cannot live here." She blocked the doorway, in case the motley pair decided to rush her, though the redoubtable Reba didn't look up to rushing anything. "There are kennels, you know."

Briny reached down and scratched the hound's head. She looked up at him, her rheumy eyes filled with adoration. "Oh, no, ma'am. I couldn't leave Reba with strangers. I understand if you're not an animal lover, Miss Burrell, but my dog and I are a team. C'mon, girl, let's go back to the hotel." He picked up his ancient suitcase and turned to go.

"Wait!" She would live to regret offering these two a temporary home. But she didn't want Tucker to think she was one of those promise breakers he held in such contempt. "Is she housebroken?"

"Sure thing. Reba's trained. And quiet as a mouse, too. She's so old, she mostly just sleeps. You'll never know she's around."

"I don't know about that." Dorian sniffed. "She reeks to high heaven."

"I guess the old girl *could* use a bath." Tucker placed one hand on the doorjamb and swayed toward Dorian with a wide grin. "There's nothing like a warm tub of bubbles to make a female smell good."

She flung open the door and stepped back, to escape his thought-numbing nearness, and put an end to the unwelcome vision of *him* in a bubble bath. "Oh, stay, Mr. Tucker," she said with resignation. "I wouldn't want to come between a boy and his dog."

He shook his head. "I can't seem to get used to answering to Mr. Tucker. Since we'll be living in each other's hip pocket, I'd sure appreciate you calling me Briny."

She wrinkled her nose in distaste. "I'm sorry. I can't, in good conscience, do that."

"Why not?"

"Because Briny is not an acceptable name."

"What do you mean?" He stepped closer, his smiling face darkened by a frown, like a cloud passing over on a sunny day.

Dorian backed up. He had an exasperating way of invading her personal space. "For one thing, Briny simply is not suitable for a man in your position. It's a good name for a child. Or for the buffoon in the double-wide you mentioned yesterday. But not for a man of substance."

His frown melted, replaced by a wounded-puppy look. Dorian's throat tightened with an unfamiliar urge to reassure him, but she didn't know how. She had little experience with compassion. Life had taught her to inflict hurt, but she didn't know how to soothe the pain she caused. So why did she feel like she'd just kicked old Reba in the ribs?

She was being ridiculous. She had accepted a job which came with responsibilities. One of which was speaking plainly even if doing so seemed harsh. "Briny is a cartoon character's name," she told him. "Do you understand why it simply won't do?"

"Not really."

"Is there another name you can adopt? We can invent one if we have to."

"Funny," he said softly. "I always figured the good a man did in the world was more important than what he called himself."

"Your name is the first impression people have of you," she explained. "You do want to make a favorable impression, don't you?"

He nodded, but was clearly unconvinced. "Well, my mama named me Brindon Zachary Tucker. That's Brindon with an *i* not an *e*."

"Hmm."

"I gotta tell you though, no one has called me that since she died quite a few years ago."

"Brindon?" Dorian tried out the sound, repeating the name several times until she could visualize it splashed across the society pages of the Dallas Morning News. "Brindon Z. Tucker. Yes. That will do. Briny is gone forever. From now on, you're to answer to Brindon and nothing else."

He shrugged. "I don't see what difference a name makes, but you're the one with all the experience living on the upper crust. Since I'm paying you good money to whip me into shape, I won't argue the matter."

"Good. We'll get along much better if you don't."

"Since we're getting so friendly, do I get to call you Dori?"

She chuckled dryly. "No one has ever called me Dori."

"Not even your mama?"

"Especially not my mama." He had an exasperating way of cutting through conventions. Why would he want to give her a cutesy nickname when no one had ever done so before? "Sit down, make yourself comfortable. It'll take me a while to get ready." She eyed the melancholy Reba who promptly made *herself* comfortable by collapsing on the floor at her master's feet. "I'll set up an appointment with a dog groomer, and we can drop her off on our way."

"Nice place you got here." He turned in a slow circle, taking in the airy apartment decorated in the bright French-country style she loved.

"Thank you." Brindon looked even more masculine among the dried hydrangeas, the blue-and-white porcelain plates, the antique furniture and the chintz fabrics than he had in Malcolm's office.

"On our way to where?" His curiosity was mild for a man about to embark on a life-altering adventure.

"Our first stop is Neiman's to pick you up a few casual things from the racks." She eyed the toned, hard-muscled length of his legs encased in tight denim. His turn around the apartment had provided her a nerve-jangling view of his body. He might have a little too much hair, but he possessed a physique male underwear models would envy.

"What are you? A forty-two long?" she asked. He nodded. "I made an appointment with a tailor for later in the week.

Having your measurements taken will save time when we visit
the designers for suits and tuxedos.''

"Tuxedos? As in more than one?''

"You'll need a variety of evening wear for different occasions. I assume you don't own formal clothes.''

"A corduroy sports coat is about as formal as I ever got.
And that was just for weddings and funerals.''

"You'll need black tie, white tie.'' She surveyed him with
a critical eye that quickly turned appreciative. With his wide
chest, broad shoulders and trim hips and waist, he was the
kind of man designers had in mind when they sat down to
create. He'd look so good when she got through with him,
rich bored women would close in on him like sharks on chum.

An image she found particularly disturbing. "Yes, you'll
definitely do justice to designer clothes.''

"I don't really need specially made stuff. Do I? Can't we
just go to the mall and pick up some duds?''

Her gaze swept over his snug, faded-to-white-in-all-the-
right-places jeans and plain cotton shirt, stiffly starched by the
hotel laundry. Tucker looked comfortable in those clothes, so
who was she to try and change him? Oh, right. She was his
highly paid image consultant.

"Lesson number two. Clothes make the man. Buying from
chain stores may be what you're accustomed to, but millionaires do not shop in malls. Walking the walk and talking the
talk are not enough. You have to look the part.'' He had to
sound the part, too, but they'd work on the drawl later.

His piercing blue gaze met and held hers. "So what you're
saying is, wearing fancy clothes will make people take me
more seriously?''

Put that way, the idea sounded absurd. But Brindon's raw,
what-you-see-is-what-you-get honesty went against everything
Dorian believed in. "Of course.''

"Whatever you say.'' He cocked his head to one side like
a curious cocker spaniel, and his bright eyes widened as if
he'd just noticed she was naked under the thin robe. A chiv-
alrous blush tinged his tan cheeks, which only made Dorian
more conscious of her careless state of dishabille. She shivered

and her nipples hardened as she turned away. She should have grabbed her thick, chenille robe. Unless he had superpowers, he couldn't see through *that.*

"What else you got planned for me today?" His words rolled over her like warm honey. An easy grin spread from his lips to his eyes. How could a grown man look both innocent and provocative at the same time?

Or maybe she had imagined the provocative part. Dorian swallowed hard, unnerved by a fleeting fantasy of luring the newly christened Brindon's blushing, work-hardened, testosterone-riddled body into her four-poster canopy bed and having her way with him on cool Egyptian cotton sheets.

Repeatedly.

Lord! Where had that come from? She shook her head, hoping to banish the lascivious thoughts from her mind. This was ridiculous and not like her at all. Nothing, no one, had excited her for a very long time.

"You do have plans for me, don't you?"

His question snapped her back to the moment, but she couldn't look him in the eye after that steamy little scenario. "After a quick stop at the mall, we're off to Emilio's."

She'd called the exclusive suburban day spa and salon the day before, alerting the talented staff to clear their schedules and man the battle stations. She was bringing them a challenge, a client to sorely test their professional makeover skills.

"Emilio's, huh? What's that? A Mexican restaurant?" Brindon settled among the cushions on one of the overstuffed sunshine-colored sofas. He stretched both arms along the back and braced a booted foot across his knee. "'Cause I could sure go for some chili *rellenos.*"

Right. Dorian expelled a deep breath. What in heaven's name had she gotten herself into? How was she going to survive ninety days with this man? "Sorry, but Emilio's is not a restaurant."

"What is it, then?" He looked up, his blue eyes so trusting she wanted to urge him to flee before she succeeded at her job and changed him, and his life, forever.

"A surprise." Dorian dashed for the relative safety of her

dressing room and ducked inside before she could blurt out the warning screaming in her mind.

How could she explain a day spa to an innocent like Tucker? She'd thought the hard part would be getting him to sit still for his first manicure. But justifying the transformation of a rare, sweetly honorable man into another rich, jaded playboy was worse.

Obviously, when she'd signed the devil's contract, she'd underestimated the consequences.

For both of them.

Chapter Three

Emilio's was definitely not a restaurant. The fancy sign out front proclaimed Luxury Day Spa and Urban Retreat. Briny wasn't sure what that meant, but instinct warned this was not a place he cared to visit.

Even for a day.

He bit back his protests. What did he know? Dorian was the expert in these matters. He should shut up and let her do her job, just as he had at the ritzy department store, where she'd turned out to be a regular force of nature. Without ever looking at a price tag, she'd ripped through racks of menswear like a Texas tornado through a trailer park, tossing one of these and two of those into the arms of a shell-shocked sales clerk who'd had to run to keep up with her. Having never seen shopping turned into an Olympic event, Briny had watched in dazed admiration. Of course, Dorian had assumed he was practicing his knot-on-a-fence-post routine.

He followed her inside the spa, lugging shopping bags filled with clothes he never would have bought on his own. He tried not to gawk, but the place was a marvel of sunshine and glass. There were enough plants under the domed skylight to put a rain forest out of business. It even sounded like a jungle. A gurgling brook, spanned by a wooden bridge and stocked with spotted koi, wound through the lobby.

Exotic birdcalls cackled and cawed from speakers hidden among the vegetation. Real parrots and cockatoos would have been too authentic, too messy for this perfect, fake environment.

"What *is* this place?" he asked.

Dorian didn't bother checking in with the girl at the desk. She set her purse strap firmly on her shoulder and took off down a long corridor, seeming to know exactly where she was going. Briny had no choice but to follow, which allowed him to admire the feminine sway of her determined, stay-out-of-my-way walk. "This is the first stop on your journey toward self-actualization," she said over her shoulder.

"Humph." He didn't believe in that self-actualization mumbo jumbo. He might not be Mr. Suave, but he wasn't Mr. Stupid. He knew exactly who he was and what he wanted. Not only that, he usually knew what other people wanted, too. Growing up in a rough-and-tumble home for "troubled youths" had put a fine point on his character-judgment skills.

This time his instincts had let him down. He couldn't quite get a handle on Ms. Dorian Burrell. Who was she? And what did she want besides the thirty thousand dollars he'd agreed to pay her? Perplexed, he watched the heir apparent of Chaco Oil traipse down the hall as if it was her own personal Paris catwalk. Did that kind of confidence come from having everything and working for nothing? Or could the skill be studied and acquired? He wanted to think so, but merely being who she was entitled her to privileges he would never have, no matter how much money he had in the bank.

He wanted to understand her self-assurance. And he wanted to possess it. He'd tried to figure her out, but the more time he spent with her, the more confused he became.

Earlier, when he had arrived at her apartment, she'd looked as pretty and wholesome as a tall sunflower. She'd seemed approachable in that little robe, with her feet bare and her head wrapped in a towel. He had been jolted into an unexpected awareness of her soft, womanly side.

Theirs was a business arrangement, so getting a bed's-eye view of the petroleum princess's lingerie so early in the game had been unsettling. But not nearly as unsettling as the sudden urge to pull her into his arms and stroke her freshly scrubbed, flower-scented skin. For a moment he'd been hypnotized into believing she really could be a girl named Dori, a girl who could learn to care for a man named Briny.

That illusion had been shattered when she emerged from her room an hour later. She'd slipped back into her glamour armor, complete with poufed hair and artfully made-up face. The sunflower was gone, replaced by a rare orchid that should be admired but never touched. Her butter-colored, ultrachic silk suit had "hands off" written all over it. Hard diamonds flashed a warning at her ears and around her neck. Even the heels on her shoes were sharp enough to pierce a man's heart.

Unlike Dori, Ms. Dorian would not take kindly to cuddling.

"If you rearrange the letters in spa," he observed with a self-amused chuckle, "you spell sap." He hoped being here didn't make him one.

"Very interesting." Her tone belied the words. She kept checking her watch as if running to catch a plane.

Briny glanced around and his voice tightened in accusation. "This is a beauty parlor, right?" With its white columns and green marble, Emilio's looked nothing like Dixie's Glama-rama back in Slapdown. But if he checked behind the ornate, gold-handled doors, he bet he would find a hidden stash of hair dryers and shampoo sinks.

Dorian scoffed. "No. It's not a beauty parlor. A spa is a gentle oasis of relaxation and tranquility, where the body and spirit can be renewed."

"All well and good. But what the heck *is* this place?"

She sighed in exasperation. "It's a little like Fluffy Pups, okay? Except for humans."

He groaned. He was no longer in the real world where most things made sense. He was stuck in Rich Land where not much of anything did. At Fluffy Pups he'd seen fat dogs trotting on treadmills, while others lolled around a big-screen television watching videos of squirrels scampering up trees. A few wore paper party hats and lapped up bowls of ice cream, enjoying what the attendant had called a birthday celebration.

Briny counted many dog lovers among his friends, but didn't know a single person who gave their pets ice-cream parties. Poor old Reba had looked as out of place among that pack of beribboned froufrou dogs as he felt in this it's-not-really-a-beauty-parlor joint.

"I've already had a bath today." He stopped walking and Dorian continued down the corridor alone, hurrying as much as her tight skirt and high heels allowed. He was willing to go along to get along, but a man had to draw the line somewhere. "I don't think I need to be here."

She stopped in her tracks, then spoke without turning around. "Of course you need to be here. Do you have any idea how hard I worked to set this up? Now, come along."

He dropped the shopping bags and folded his arms across his chest. Just because he'd agreed to let her be the boss didn't mean she had to act so darned bossy. "Not until I know exactly where we're going and what we're gonna do when we get there."

She marched back to him, all five feet ten inches of her pulled into the exasperated pose of a weary mother dealing with her stubborn child. "After I place you in the very capable hands of Mr. Emilio himself, I have to zip off to a stuffy old Art League meeting. But I'll be back in time to take you to dinner."

"What about lunch?" he asked warily. "Where I come from, we sit down to at least three meals a day."

"They'll serve you something."

"When?"

"Between treatments."

"What do I need to be treated for? I'm not sick." Uncouthness wasn't a disease in west Texas, but it could be in Dallas. Dorian seemed to think the lack of refinement was contagious.

Before she could answer, a little man in a leopard-skin-print silk shirt, tight black leather pants and high-heeled boots swooped out of nowhere. Tiny gold earrings dangled from both ears. He let out a squeak and clasped one hand to his heart when he spotted them.

"Dorian, darling, it's so good to see you." He smeared her hand with noisy kisses. "You're looking exceptionally ravishing today." He turned to Briny. "And what have we here? Oh, my, you are a brawny one, aren't you?"

Dorian hurried the introductions. "Emilio, this is Brindon Tucker, the, ah, gentleman I told you about. Brindon, Mr. Emilio is the best in the business. He's a makeover wizard and has promised to give you a whole new look."

Mr. Emilio was definitely not a barber. Briny extended his hand warily, hoping the fella wouldn't feel obliged to slobber on it. "Nice to meet you."

"Believe me," Emilio gushed. "The pleasure is all mine."

Briny extracted his hand and turned to Dorian. He'd spent years trying to turn an unwanted, scabby-kneed kid into a decent man. He thought he'd done a pretty fair job, too, but the woman he'd hired to apply the finishing touches obviously found more than his manners lacking. Her job was to overhaul his social skills, not change who he was. He'd tolerated her rejecting his name, but enlisting this poofy little man to make him look like somebody else was going too far.

"What's wrong with how I look?" he demanded. No one had ever objected to his Billy Ray hairstyle or cowhand mustache before.

"Nothing if you were the new front man for the Sons of the Pioneers!" Emilio struck what could only be called a pose and examined his latest assignment from head to toe. "Hmm. Dorian, dear, you were so right. I certainly do have my work cut out for me. But, oh, the possibilities!"

"I'm in a rush," she said. "Just work one of your miracles on him."

"Do you have a particular look in mind?"

"Yes." She sighed. "Rich."

"And dangerous?" The spa man smirked. "I love doing dangerous."

"Think polished. Old money."

"Casual elegance?"

"If you can manage that, you truly are a wizard."

"Whoa!" Briny resisted being nudged forward like a shy child at a recital. "Don't I have any say in this?"

"No," she answered.

"Did you just say no?"

She glanced at her watch again, and her face wrinkled in displeasure. "That's right, Mr. Tucker. I said no. You have heard the word before, haven't you? Or are you used to having women back in Slapdown sigh 'yes, yes, yes,' as they melt into puddles at your feet?" Her tone indicated his dubious charm could not possibly work outside his small town. Or on her.

"I haven't had to melt too many," he allowed. "Most of the time they're willing."

"That's what I am." She adjusted her purse strap again. "I am ready and willing to fulfill my end of the bargain. But the question is, are you willing to let me do that?"

"Yes, but I don't see how—"

"You hired me to teach you how to swim in deep water. I can't teach you anything if you won't wear the regulation life vest."

He shook his head, amazed at how quickly her line of reasoning could leave him in the dust. "What are you talking about?"

This time she did more than nudge. Before Briny could brace himself, she pushed him into the outstretched arms of the makeover man. "He's all yours. You boys have fun."

"Yum!" Emilio's appreciative look made Briny do a quick two-step. *Now* he had something to be nervous about.

Dorian sighed. "I know I'm giving you a sow's ear, Emilio. But when I return I expect to find a silk purse."

"I do love a challenge."

Briny bristled. "Where I come from, a sow's ear would be a lot more practical."

"This isn't where you come from," Dorian pointed out archly.

Put firmly in his place, Briny was about to ask what the

transformation procedures would entail, but didn't get the chance.

"Your wish is my command, darling." Emilio bowed and rolled his hand at Dorian in an exaggerated Ali Baba show of obeisance.

She checked the time again and uttered a girly curse. "Oh, great! Now I'm late. Make sure he gets the full treatment, everything from the toenails up. Here are his new clothes." She scooped the shopping bags off the floor and shoved them into Emilio's arms. "I'll be back by six. *Ciao!*"

"You're not leaving me here, are you?" Briny was in uncharted territory and didn't know the trail. That's why he'd hired Dorian. She rolled her eyes at his question, making him feel as abandoned as Reba had looked when he handed her over to the doggie spa attendant.

"Don't whine," Dorian scolded.

"I never whine." In his experience, the squeaky wheel got the most lickings and demerits. He'd learned at an early age the truth about attracting more flies with honey than with vinegar.

Their gazes locked for a long moment, and her expression softened. He thought he might have glimpsed a flicker of compassion in her dark eyes, but it was gone before he could be sure. For the first time since they'd met yesterday, she looked at him like a person and not a project.

She quickly averted her gaze, retreating behind her armor. "I have to run. I'm expected to put in an appearance at the Art League meeting and can't get out of the obligation. Burrells have always supported the arts."

Briny wished he had some gum. Or a beer. Something to ease the tension coiled in his mind and muscles. "Well, I guess if you have the family honor to uphold, I can manage on my own." Which would be nothing new. He had been on his own since he was seven years old.

"Of course you can," she said. "Prepare to be pampered. I've ordered the VIP treatment all the way. Ordinarily, a booking here takes weeks to get, but Emilio was a sweetheart and squeezed you in."

"Anything for you, Dorian, dear."

"I really need to go. Emilio, take care of him now. Ta!"

"Oh, it'll be my pleasure."

Briny watched her turn and rush down the corridor, her tall, thin heels clicking on the fake-marble floor. She was unlike any woman he'd ever known.

She might act cool and bored, but there was an appealing softness beneath her calculated indifference. Most people probably didn't take the time to see the vulnerability she tried so desperately to hide.

"Oh!" She stopped and spun around. "Emilio! Don't forget to feed him. He may get hungry." She clicked on for a few more steps, then stopped again when additional instructions popped into her mind. "Go with less hair." Her finger fluttered under her nose. "And let's lose the cowboy cookie duster."

Briny stroked his overgrown mustache protectively and glanced at the sly-eyed Emilio with trepidation. A guy who shaved his head as smooth as a billiard ball might have the wrong idea about what Dorian considered *less*. "Just so you know, bub, I happen to like my hair."

"Yes, I can see that." Emilio linked arms with his potential masterpiece. "Ooh. Muscles, too. Nice." He led the way through a bamboo-detailed door at the end of the hall and into a sunlit room furnished with a bubbling fountain, towering ficus trees and a sheet-draped massage table.

Once inside, Emilio propped both hands on his hips and turned to Briny with a big grin. "Now. What do you say we get you out of those clothes?"

Three hours latter, wearing nothing but a towel, Briny was escorted from the sauna by a woman named Sydney who was ready to begin his next treatment. He didn't dare ask. He'd already fallen victim to something called a shiatsu massage, an impressive form of torture named, in his opinion, with too many vowels.

After that he'd been subjected to the fifty-minute deluxe aromatherapy experience, kneaded like bread dough and oiled down until he smelled like a six-foot, five-inch stick of incense. Then there was the deep-heat boreh scrub. Another massage lady had slathered his body with a paste made of jojoba oil, rice powder, sandalwood, tumeric, and enough cinnamon, cloves and nutmeg to bake a dozen pumpkin pies. The powerful scent had launched his stomach into rumbling overdrive. In the craziest moment of the craziest day of his life so far, she had finished by rubbing him down with gloppy handfuls of grated carrots.

After showering and moisturizing, he'd slipped into a velvety robe and sandals, like something the Queen of Sheba might have worn to a chariot race. He'd been escorted out to the terrace where he joined a group of ladies, all dressed in the same robes and sandals, for lunch. At least that's what the waiter called it. Briny wasn't sure a bowl of "baby arugula tossed with grilled tomatoes and pine nuts and lightly misted with olive oil" actually qualified as lunch. Starving, he'd taken the man at his word. But after scarfing down every limp leaf in the bowl, he was still hungry.

"I think you're going to enjoy the stone therapy, Mr. Tucker." Sydney, the massage technician urged him into a reclining chair. "Are you familiar with the procedure?"

"Not really. And I don't have enough imagination to guess." Thankfully, this was a day spa, and the day was nearly over. He'd had just about all the self-actualization he could take. He climbed into the chair with a long sigh of resignation, feeling as naked in his terry loincloth as a baby jaybird. Fortunately, the staff didn't seem to notice their clients' state of undress.

Dorian had better have a good reason for throwing him on the mercy of Mr. Emilio and his smock-clad minions. She obviously considered the treatments a crucial part of his self-improvement program. Maybe she thought she could relate to him better if he looked more like the type of men she was used to. Sandal-wearing men who felt comfortable having avocado facials.

But he'd do what he had to do to connect with Dorian. He wasn't crazy about what he was being put through, but he'd just cowboy up and tough things out. All his life he'd been an all-or-nothing kind of guy who, once committed, did not back down or give up. He'd spent eleven years working on oil rigs and supervising roughnecks. He could take anything these New Age nutcases dished out and come up smelling like…patchouli.

Sydney explained the treatment. "First I'll rub your feet with essential oils, then I'll insert hot stones between your toes. After placing warm, green-tea poultices over your eyes, I'll ask you to relax to the soothing sounds of crashing waves and classical music while everything cools."

"Pardon me for saying so, ma'am, but that doesn't sound at all pleasant."

Not to a sow's ear reluctant to become a silk purse.

She smiled. "Your gratification is guaranteed."

He settled back in the chair. He might never get the hang of being a rich man. When he was poor, he'd worn steel-toed boots to avoid stepping on hot rocks. Now that he had money, he had to pay a gal in a pink coat to poke them between his toes. Wasn't that called irony? He'd ask Dorian so they'd have something to talk about over dinner.

"Whatever you say." He kept thinking how she'd dropped him off with the same detachment she'd shown when they'd left Reba at the dog washer. She acted as if she didn't need to explain anything because he was too dense to understand. That hurt. But at least her behavior put things in perspective. Despite that little Dori fantasy he'd indulged in back at her apartment, he could never be more to her than a job.

Sydney checked her clipboard. "I see you're scheduled for a seaweed wrap and body polishing before your manicure and pedicure, Mr. Tucker. Then it's off to the esthetician for deep-pore cleansing. Last stop, Mr. Emilio's salon."

"Oh, good. I'd hate to miss any of the fun." A luxury day spa was clearly something a crazy person dreamed up for ladies with too much money and time on their hands. Except for the waiter and chirpy Mr. Emilio, he was the only male on the premises. Lordy, if his friends back in Slapdown ever got wind of how he'd spent the day, he would never live down the embarrassment.

The foot rub wasn't half-bad, but Briny tensed as he watched Sydney use long tongs to lift heated stones out of what looked like a hibachi. She wedged the smooth stones between his toes, and the deep heat radiated through his body. Surprisingly enough, the treatment felt good.

"Close your eyes." He did, and she covered them with what looked like limp tea bags. "Let the heat and music work their magic," she crooned in a soothing voice. "Relax from the inside out. Allow yourself to be transported to a higher plane where you become one with light and warmth."

Briny tried but felt ridiculous with tea bags on his eyelids and rocks between his toes. For the life of him, he couldn't figure out how being wrapped in seaweed or having his pores steam-cleaned would make him a better man. He didn't agree with Dorian's tactics, but a born-rich person was bound to look at things differently than someone who'd had a pile of money dropped on his unsuspecting head.

Doubt stabbed him in the gut. He hoped trusting her wasn't a mistake. O'Neal had assured him of her qualifications, but he hadn't really listened once he'd heard a beautiful young woman was willing to sign a contract to spend time with him. Under ordinary circumstances, Dorian Burrell would not have given Briny Tucker, oil rig crew foreman, the time of day. Brindon Z. Tucker, multimillionaire, might play in her ballpark, but he still had a way to go.

If he quit worrying and rolled with the punches, everything would work out. He just needed to restate his objectives to make sure Dorian knew what he wanted. Over dinner he would remind her that his goal was to acquire the knowledge and confidence he needed to make his mark on the world, not to achieve smoother, more supple skin.

Briny squirmed in the recliner, ready for the hellish spa day to end, yet knowing he had several more hours—and Mr. Emilio's so-called miracle—to endure. Even if he'd been a give-up guy by nature, he couldn't escape now. He was dressed in a towel and had no idea what had become of his clothes.

Sydney noticed his restless movements and began to chant

again. "Relax. Release the stress. Let yourself become one with the light and the warmth."

Right. His stomach rumbled, protesting the rabbit food he'd eaten for lunch. He didn't have anything against light and warmth. But what he really wanted to become one with was a big, juicy T-bone steak.

"Darling, come in and sit down." Emilio jumped up from his cluttered desk and welcomed Dorian into the gilt-edged styling salon. He snapped his fingers, and a shampoo girl scurried forth with a tray and offered Dorian a tiny glass of Campari.

Accepting the liqueur, she took a small sip. "I know. I'm late." Never apologize, never explain. Always a good rule to live by. "If you have the bill ready, I'll sign so you can fax it to Malcolm O'Neal's office. He's handling Tucker's expenses."

Emilio tapped a few computer keys, and a piece of paper rolled out of the printer. He presented the invoice with a flourish. A less worldly person would have gasped at the expense incurred during a single day spent in his establishment, but Dorian was well-aware of the high cost of self-actualization. She scribbled her name across the bottom without bothering to read the itemized statement.

"Well, where is he? Bring him out, and we'll be on our way."

"No, *non, nein, nyet.*" Emilio ushered her over to a lush eggplant-colored sofa piled with pillows. "Sit, dear. Relax."

"I can't. I'm in a hurry."

"You're always in a hurry." Emilio placed his hands on her shoulders and gently pushed her down. "Sit. I will not take no for answer."

She sat, not realizing how tired she was until she collapsed among the silken pillows. When the interminable Art League meeting had finally ended, she'd driven by Fluffy Pups to pick up Tucker's horrible old dog, which admittedly did smell better. Later, when she had stepped out of the shower, she'd found the pony-size hound curled up asleep on the floor beside her bed. All she could think about was the damage the dog could do to her white carpet. Tucker had better be right about his pet being housebroken. If not, there would be hell to pay.

She'd freshened her makeup, twisted her hair into a chignon and slipped into a little black dress suitable for a quiet dinner in a posh restaurant. On the way to Emilio's, she'd called and secured an eight-o'clock reservation at her favorite West End watering hole. Tucker had been unhappy when she had left him, and Emilio's ministrations and trademark low-fat, low-cal, low-taste luncheon had probably not improved his mood. Unless she missed her guess, a big slab of beef would smooth his ruffled feathers. She could feed him, and provide his first etiquette lesson, in a painless nonthreatening fashion. She loved killing two birds with one stone.

She was surprised to see so many of the spa's massage techs, stylists, pore specialists and manicurists still at work past six. On second thought, maybe they weren't working at all. They were just lurking around, like a restless crowd at a concert, awaiting the opening act.

"What's going on?"

Emilio braced a fist on one hip and gave her a triumphant smile. "A miracle has been wrought here today." His expansive gesture took in the room of smiling staffers. "We have worked like pyramid-building slaves to transform your sow's ear into a fine Cordovan leather purse. Silk just wasn't his style," he added as an aside.

"And I appreciate your efforts, but—"

"No buts!" He waved his hand to shush her protests. "The viewing of a masterpiece should not be undertaken lightly. That is why the Mona Lisa is exhibited at the Louvre and not in the drive-through window of your local bank."

Emilio's enthusiasm was contagious, and Dorian smiled.

"Sip your Campari, my dear, and prepare to be amazed."

Buzzing around in his high-heeled boots like a magician setting the stage for his greatest illusion, Emilio motioned for someone to replace the classical relaxation music with a hard-driving rock beat. Unseen hands dimmed the overhead lights.

"Emilio, I appreciate everything you've done, but this, ah, excess really isn't necessary."

"But excess is key, my dear. You know quite well, presentation is everything."

True. Presentation *was* everything. Another rule she lived by. One thing Dorian had learned from her absentee mother was that appearances were far more important than feelings. Appearances could be orchestrated and controlled. Feelings were…messy. Cupping the glass of nerve-settling liqueur in both hands, Dorian relaxed against the sumptuous cushions. Wouldn't hurt to give the beauty guru his moment. No doubt he'd earned it.

"Are you ready?" Emilio called over the music.

She nodded, a queen preparing to review the troops. "Yes. I believe I am ready to behold a wonder." She laughed, caught up in the excitement of the unveiling. Her stomach, warmed by another sip of alcohol, fluttered at the prospect of seeing Brindon again.

What was she thinking? She was simply curious to see what Emilio had accomplished. How Brindon would look in the clothes she'd selected. She'd chosen with care, picking fabrics and styles to complement his long, muscular frame. Muted colors to show off the deep blue of his eyes, his bronzed skin and the dark richness of his hair. Her interest was not in the man, but in the results of her handiwork.

The tingling anticipation was no more than professional interest.

So why had the enigmatic west Texan invaded her wandering thoughts during today's long, dry meeting? While the Art League president droned on about the autumn fund-raiser, Dorian had speculated about her new employer and the job she had accepted. A job that had seemed simple enough coming from Malcolm. All she had to do was teach the new millionaire some social skills, polish off his rough edges, and connect him with people who could help him learn to manage his new lifestyle.

But, as she'd soon discovered, there was nothing simple about him. She suspected he wanted more than training in the proper way to hold a demitasse. Yesterday tutoring Tucker had seemed like an easy way to earn the cash she needed to see her through until September. A lark. But today she couldn't shake the feeling that she was involved in something important. Something big. Bigger than Tucker.

Bigger than herself.

Dorian's attention snapped back to the moment when Emilio picked up a hairbrush and began warbling like a campy beauty pageant announcer with a microphone. "Here…he…is! Mis…ter Won…derful!" Someone trained a small spotlight on a doorway hung with glittery beads.

Sydney, the massage technician, popped her fingers in her mouth and blew a long, low wolf whistle. Someone else called, "Get the show on the road!" The women began stamping their feet in rhythmic demand.

Clearly pleased with himself, the spa owner bowed, sporting a Cheshire cat grin. "And now, without further ado, I give the world the future heartthrob of the greater Dallas-Fort Worth area. The sleek, the chic, Brindon Z. Tucker!"

Dorian relaxed enough to laugh at Emilio's antics. At least *someone* had fun today. Tapping her foot and bobbing her head to the beat of heavy rock music, she focused her gaze on the spotlit area, raised the glass of liqueur to her lips and took another sip.

Urged forward by a pair of feminine hands, a man slowly parted the shiny beads and stepped through the doorway, his head lowered to block the glare from his eyes.

One look at Brindon, upgraded to version 2.0, and Dorian promptly spewed Campari in a very unladylike and highly undignified spit take.

Chapter Four

Catcalls and applause erupted when Brindon ambled to the center of the room. His bowed head and heightened color made his discomfort clearly visible. Emilio always delivered, so Dorian had fully expected to get her money's worth. Still, it was hard to believe this handsome, well-dressed fugitive from a *GQ* layout was the same man she had dropped off a few hours ago.

Gone was the unrefined roughneck who considered himself dressed up in pressed jeans. In his place was a sleek, polished, gorgeous hunk of ultrafashionable masculinity. Dorian noticed the other women eyeing him with unconcealed lust and had to admit what they—and Emilio—obviously knew. With all his rough, west-Texas Briny edges smoothed, new millionaire philanthropist Brindon Z. Tucker was to-die-for.

A smooth shave and rakish new haircut thrust the rugged planes of his face into sharp relief. Apparently, she hadn't really seen him before. For the first time she noticed his high cheekbones, the straight blade of his nose. Had those temptingly full lips been there all along, buried beneath bristly facial hair like treasure beneath the sea? Amazing. Her startled gaze raked down his Armani-clad body to the expensive Prada boots she had selected, and back up to his self-conscious expression. She'd purchased the casual yet sophisticated clothes fearing they would wear the man, instead of the other way around.

Boy, had she been wrong. The charcoal triple-front-pleated slacks and matching cotton cashmere pullover fit his tall, muscular body as if they had been cut and sewn to his specific measurements—his quite impressive measurements. The dark fabric intensified his exotic coloring, giving him a look that was both mysterious and dangerous.

Seductive.

Brindon's unforgettably blue eyes met hers, and his lips tilted up in a slow, hope-you're-happy grin. He cocked one brow and held her gaze for a long moment, as though challenging her to find fault with him now. How could she, when he was sartorial perfection on the hoof?

He winked, and a powerful emotion unfurled within Dorian that revved her pulse and squeezed her heart, then suffused her with incredible warmth. Surely that ripple of pleasure was appreciation of Emilio's efforts and the improbable transformation. Had to be. Attraction was not acceptable. Neither was its dastardly evil twin, desire.

Such feelings were inappropriate in a business arrangement and would only get her into trouble. Like the wayward animal urges that had ambushed her earlier, they must be nipped in the bud.

Emilio stamped his foot. "Don't just sit there, Dorian. Say something."

He popped a tissue from a box and fluttered it at her. "Words. I need words. Wipe the drool off your mouth, darling, and tell me what you think."

What did she think? How *could* she think? What with a clamoring physical awareness and the disturbing suspicion that her powerful reaction indicated an innate superficiality on her part, she could barely entertain a coherent thought. She reminded herself the man hadn't changed. Beneath the designer clothes and trendy haircut, he was still a lucky lottery winner from a place called Slapdown. He might as well hail from another planet for all they had in common. Only his appearance was different.

But weren't appearances everything? Or were they meaningless, as Brindon seemed to think? Funny, she couldn't remember. To her mother, maintaining a veneer of flawless superiority took precedence over caring about things. Or people. Dorian didn't like to think she had anything in common with a woman who'd rarely thrown a scrap of affection to her only child, but hadn't Granny Pru accused her of adopting Cassandra's values as her own?

To cover her bewilderment and buy a few seconds to regain control of her runaway emotions, Dorian leaned forward on the sofa, her hands clasped in her lap. "Congratulations," she said to Emilio in her trademark throw-the-serfs-a-crumb tone. "Well done."

"Is that all you can say?" Emilio's petulance indicated her words were not generous enough to feed his vast ego.

"I had my doubts," she allowed. "But like Rumpelstiltskin of fairy-tale fame, you have achieved the impossible by spinning straw into gold."

The salon owner gave Brindon's rear end a light pat. "Strut your stuff, B, let her see you in motion."

Brindon pulled away from the effusive stylist, his grin giving way to annoyance. "That's enough," he drawled. "You're making me feel like a slab of beef on Sizzler's all-you-can-eat night."

Dorian cringed. So much for illusion. Next order of business, a dialect coach to remove the aw-shucks cadence from his speech.

Emilio turned to his staff. "You heard the man. Fun's over. Run along. Shoo!" The women cast final, longing looks toward Brindon before filing out.

"Women!" Emilio snorted with derision. "They can be so obvious!"

Brindon's tanned finger stroked his upper lip where the mustache used to be. Dorian found the gesture maddeningly sensual. "Do I look as nekkid as I feel?"

Emilio expelled a loud dramatic breath. "No. But more's the pity."

Brindon ignored his comment and sat on the sofa beside

Dorian. "Tell me the truth, Miss Burrell. I trust your opinion. Do I look funny?"

Dorian breathed in the scent of the cologne she'd selected. Spicy and woodsy, with an engaging hint of lotus and musk. He smelled like heaven. "No." The word was so breathy, she cleared her throat to try again. "You don't look funny at all. I think you look…" She paused, distracted by the earnestness in his piercing blue gaze.

"Like I'm trying to be something I'm not?" He slapped his knee. "I knew it. That's what you were going to say, right?"

"No. You look…" What could she say and be truthful? Good enough to eat? Drop-dead gorgeous? Her heartbeat kicked up another notch. Better not go there. "Fine. I was going to say, you look just fine."

"Really?" His voice registered doubt. "Because these clothes feel a little girly to me. I'm not used to wearing stuff like this." He stuck out his arm. "Here, feel how soft this shirt is."

Her hand brushed over his arm. The expensive fabric floated lightly over the steely muscles beneath. Touching him intensified his effect on her, and she immediately regretted doing so. "It's cotton cashmere. It's supposed to be soft."

"So you don't think I look like a big phony?" He raked one hand through his freshly shorn hair.

"Not at all." She jumped to her feet to escape his intoxicating scent, the too-tempting heat of his all-male body. "Emilio, I didn't think you could pull this off. I apologize for doubting you."

The salon owner dropped a mock curtsy. "An artist never settles for less than perfection."

"Thank you, I think." Brindon extended his hand, and Emilio gave it a delicate shake. "I'll get my new duds." Brindon disappeared through the beaded curtain and returned with the bulging shopping bags. "Let's get out of here. Somewhere in Dallas there has to be a steak with my name on it."

Dorian smiled. He didn't even realize how wonderful he looked, which only added to his charm. Accustomed to men so vain they used women to track their sex appeal like a Dow

Jones commodity, she found Brindon's artlessness refreshing and delightful.

"I thought you might say that, so I made dinner reservations." Despite the emotional turmoil he'd caused, she was hungry, too. For food. At least that was one need she did not have to hide.

Briny sat in the dimly lit, plant-cluttered restaurant and listened as carefully as a student anticipating a pop quiz, while Dorian went over the complicated wine list. He had no idea there were so many different kinds, or that wine could be so obscenely expensive. He was only familiar with the stuff his buddies called "fruit of the vine" and served from boxes and jugs at parties. He'd seen the cork-sniffing, mouth-swishing routine in movies, but had never dreamed someday he would be seated in a fancy joint telling a snooty wine steward he found the vintage acceptable.

Dorian walked him through the ritual. After the man left, she explained why her choice, a dark Bordeaux with a French-sounding name, complemented the chateaubriand she had selected for their entrée.

"So there's more to this wine thing than white with chicken and red with beef?" He was careful to modulate his voice. He wanted to be heard over the quartet of string-playing musicians without sounding as if he'd been raised in a sawmill.

She nodded. "I'll get you a book, and you can read up on the subject, if you'd like."

"Seems like the more I learn, the more I realize how much I don't know. After today I feel like I crawled out from under a rock."

"You're doing fine." Quietly she pointed out his salad fork, preparing him for the arrival of the first course.

"There's that word again," he teased.

"Which word?"

"Fine. Earlier you said I looked fine. Now you say I'm doing fine. Are you sure I'm not embarrassing you? Because I would hate to do that."

"Relax. You aren't embarrassing me." She gave him an encouraging smile, and he wondered if she was just being nice.

The musicians struck up a new tune. He tipped his head in their direction. "I know what a fiddle is. But what are those other instruments?"

She discreetly pointed out the two violins, a viola and a cello. "They're playing Puccini's 'Crisantemi.'"

"How do you know that?" He didn't try to hide his amazement. Such ready knowledge was one of the things that separated them. Something he wanted.

She shrugged. "Too many years of music appreciation lessons. Oh, I picked up your dog at the groomer this afternoon. She actually seemed glad to see me."

"Reba," he prompted, "is her name. If she got half as much fussing over as I did today, I don't blame her." He studied Dorian in the candlelight. She looked pale and beautiful in her simple black dress and carefully pinned-up hair. Like the lonely princess in the castle atop the glass hill. He hadn't thought about that story for a long time. Not since his mother died and there was no one left to tuck him in and whisper fairy tales in his ear until he fell asleep. "I know I was glad to see you." Too glad.

"You were?"

In another, those words might have sounded hopeful. But why would a woman like Dorian Burrell need reassurance? Especially from him. "Yeah. I was afraid I'd have to go home with Emilio. Nice guy, but not really my type."

She laughed for the first time since he'd met her, and the sound was as musical as the wind chimes his cottage mom had hung in a tree outside the boys' room. Her laughter stirred his blood and made him long for things that could never be.

She leaned forward, her perfectly manicured hands folded properly on the tablecloth. "May I ask you a question?"

"Sure. Anything."

"Why are you doing this?"

"I'm hungry. That bowl of greens they gave me for lunch wouldn't keep a hamster alive."

"I don't mean why are you eating." She smiled. "Why are

you paying me thirty thousand dollars to teach you what you could probably learn by reading a few books?''

''I don't believe what I can learn from you can be found in books.'' Given enough time, he might figure out on his own how to dress and which wine to order, but not the rest. Not the important stuff. No book could teach him confidence, or make him feel as if deserved good things in his life.

''Why do you want to be accepted by society?'' she persisted. ''There are plenty of millionaire basketball players and movie stars just as unprepared for wealth as you say you are. They do all right.''

Replicating her pose, he folded his recently manicured hands on the table. ''I don't need to learn how to spend money, Miss Burrell. Any loose-brain fool is born knowing how to do that. What I want to learn is how to use money.''

She shook her head. ''I'm afraid I don't understand. And please, call me Dorian.''

''I'm not great at explaining myself. That's another thing I want you to teach me. Did you go to college? Dorian?''

She nodded.

''Well, I didn't. In fact, I barely managed to scrape through high school. In your school, did they have a 'Most Likely to' list?''

''Yes.'' She seemed curious where the subject might lead.

He tilted his head speculatively. ''What were you voted?''

She winced. ''Before I confess, you need to know I attended an exclusive Eastern girls' school. They didn't have designations for Best Citizen and Most Studious.''

''So what designation did you get?''

She hesitated before answering. '''Most Likely to Marry Old Money.'''

She had the good grace to look embarrassed.

''There you go.'' He frowned. ''Is old money better than new money?''

''Some people think so.''

''Do you?''

''I don't know,'' she admitted. ''My mother is still trying to break into old money cliques, but my paternal great-grandfather was the first rich man on either branch of my family tree. And that was just because he was lucky enough to drill for oil in the right place.'' She brightened. ''A little like winning the lottery.''

''Only harder and dirtier.'' He glanced at the basket of hot, yeasty rolls the waiter placed on the table, then at Dorian. ''Is it bad manners for me to help myself to a piece of that bread? I'm starving.''

''Not at all. That's what it's for.'' She demonstrated by taking a crusty roll from the napkin-lined basket, placing it on her bread plate, then slanting her butter knife across the plate's rim.

He tore his roll in two and slathered an icy pat of butter over the warm surface. Savoring the rich flavor, he closed his eyes for a moment. When he opened them, he winked at her. ''I needed that.''

She smiled and extended the basket. ''Have another.''

''Don't mind if I do.'' After a few more bites, he said, ''I started working at Chaco Oil when I was eighteen years old. It's the only job I ever had.''

''Really?'' She sounded surprised. She'd probably never considered that he was one of the many anonymous vassals who made the Burrells' feudal-lord lifestyle possible.

''In eleven years,'' he said, ''I never heard a single man bad-mouth Portis Channing.'' He told her that even though he'd never met the founder of Chaco Oil, her hardworking, kindhearted ancestor had long been his source of inspiration, providing the role model his own father could not.

''My grandmother says he was a good man,'' she told him.

''The fellas who worked for him thought he was an angel come to earth. I heard he'd give a poor man the shirt off his back.''

''Yes, he had a reputation for generosity. I regret I never knew him. He died before I was born.''

The salads arrived, and Briny emulated Dorian by carefully placing his napkin in his lap and nodding to the waiter when he'd cranked enough pepper over the plate. He watched her to make sure he picked up the correct fork. Instead of diving into the unrecognizable assortment of lightly dressed lettuce as his rumbling stomach demanded, he raised a genteel forkful to his mouth.

"Let's go back to the 'Most Likely' topic," Dorian said between bites. "I want to hear what you were voted in school."

He grinned sheepishly. "Just so you know, the boys' school I attended was *not* exclusive. Any incorrigible troublemaker could get in."

"And?"

He expelled a deep breath. "My fellow delinquents voted me 'Most Likely to Do Time.'" The way things had turned out, winning that title had been the best thing that could have happened to him. Scrupulous honesty had grown out of that low expectation.

Her eyes widened, and he hastened to explain lest she think her life was in danger. "Oh, I wasn't violent or a thief or anything like that. Just a kid with a chip on his shoulder who maybe took rebelling against authority a little too far."

"What about your parents?"

"Mom died when I was seven. My old man didn't have what the child welfare people called parenting skills. I was ten when I got to Los Huerfanos. Stayed until they cut me loose eight years later. I don't know where my father is, or even if he's still alive."

"I'm sorry." She reached across the table and laid her hand gently atop his. A flash of electricity as hot as chain lightning arced between them, and Briny could tell by the startled look in her eyes that she felt the heat, too. She yanked her hand away and thrust it into her lap as if that would negate her response.

"My daddy died thirteen years ago," she said as though nothing wonderful had just happened. "He contracted amyotrophic lateral sclerosis when he was thirty-six."

He must have looked confused, because she clarified. "Lou Gehrig's disease. Daddy lived two more years, but they weren't good years for him. Despite his illness, we were close. Or maybe we were close because of his illness. I still miss him. Like your father, my mother is no fan of parenting."

So they did have something in common. The conversation flowed from one topic to the next, and Briny marveled at how easy talking to Dorian was. He'd expected to be tongue-tied around her, but she seemed determined to put him at ease.

When the main course arrived, he was relieved that in spite of its hoity-toity French name, chateaubriand was no more than a thick tenderloin steak, grilled and served with some kind of strange sauce. Dorian said it was béarnaise, made from egg yolks and butter and flavored with shallots, wine vinegar and seasonings. He didn't know why anyone would want to ruin a perfectly good slab of beef by drowning it in fancy sauce, but he listened politely as she presented a brief sauce lesson, explaining the differences between hollandaise and bordelaise.

As the meal progressed, Briny pretended they were simply a man and a woman on a date, enjoying good food and each other's company. Too soon the evening would be over, and they'd resume their roles of hired tutor and eager pupil, separated by class distinctions that were no longer supposed to exist in America.

"I need to tell you something." He had finished his dessert, so he wiped his mouth and placed his napkin beside his plate as Dorian had done. As reluctant as he was to leave the sheltering walls of the restaurant, the meal was almost over, and he still had things to say. "I was sure you were barking up the wrong tree with this makeover stuff. In fact, I was planning to remind you tonight that there's more to my plan than having clean fingernails." He stroked his upper lip, nervously searching for the phantom mustache.

"I know that—"

"Wait. Let me finish. I started out thinking the kind of clothes I wore and the way my hair was cut didn't matter. I wanted to believe doing the right thing was what really counted."

"And?"

"I'm a big enough man to admit when I'm wrong."

"No." Her face creased in a worried frown. "Please don't let me, or anyone else, change your values." She set aside her barely touched dish of tiramisu.

"When we arrived tonight, that fella up front, the one in the monkey suit, what's he called?"

"The maître d'?" she supplied.

"Yeah, him. He didn't blink an eye when he showed us to our table."

"So?"

"So that means I look like I belong here." He glanced around to indicate the sophisticated, well-dressed, well-heeled patrons. What he really wanted to say was the maître d' had believed him a fitting escort for Dorian Burrell. "That wouldn't have happened yesterday."

She caught her lower lip between her teeth and took a deep breath. "Doing the right thing *is* what counts, Brindon. The new look is only meant to give you an edge. That's all. Don't get caught up in appearances. Trust me, it's not a good place to be."

"I never worried about what I looked like before," he told her honestly. "But I'm beginning to get a sense of how the world works. How wearing the right uniform opens doors."

"What do you mean?"

"People have expectations. Most of the time they're not willing to dig deep or look beneath the surface. If I don't appear to be what they expect, how do they know they can trust me?"

"By your actions?" she suggested.

"Nope." He shook his head. "Tell me something. If Malcolm O'Neal showed up in his office wearing a Don Ho shirt and Bermuda shorts, what would you think?"

"That he'd lost his ever-loving mind?"

"Exactly. Goes against all your expectations, right?"

"I suppose so."

"Even if he gave you the same sound financial advice, you wouldn't be so sure of him anymore, would you?"

"No. But I *would* pay to see Malcolm in Bermuda shorts." She laughed again, and the lilting sound encouraged Briny to open up.

"Most of the time, I don't think people like having their expectations challenged. Makes them uncomfortable. And above everything else, people don't want to be uncomfortable."

She looked at him closely, as though impressed by his insight. "You've given this a lot of thought."

"Yes, I have." He'd made Dorian uncomfortable when they met in O'Neal's office yesterday. Wary, she'd kept her distance, watching him as she would a snake. That's why he hadn't fussed too much during the hostile makeover. He wanted to do whatever it took to gain her acceptance and get close to her. He was making progress, because when she looked at him now he didn't think she saw a reptile who had slipped out of a skin that no longer fit. She recognized a fuzzy caterpillar, ready to change and spread its wings.

"From childhood, we're cautioned not to judge a book by the cover." Dorian sipped the coffee served with dessert. "You can't know what's inside by looking at the package. That's reason. However, human nature sometimes runs counter to reason."

"Maybe human nature is stronger than reason," he suggested. "Or maybe we just trust our experience more than we trust our hearts."

Dorian considered that for a long time before answering. "Yes, I think perhaps we do. Unfortunately."

Briny had dated girls back in Slapdown. They'd gone for beer and burgers at Whiskey Pete's, a smoky little juke joint that provided the only night life in town. They'd listened to country music while flirting and talking about people they knew, movies they'd seen. They'd shared details of their daily lives, but Briny couldn't recall ever revealing his thoughts or discussing ideas. Why? Because the girls he knew didn't expect him to have any?

Or because *he* hadn't thought he had any?

Maybe wearing fine clothes and sitting across a linen-covered table decorated with real flowers in a restaurant where musicians played Puccini made him feel like a man worthy of Dorian Burrell's attention.

But what if the clothes, the flowers and the violin music had nothing to do with how he felt? What if the woman had given him that unexpected, warm rush of confidence? He watched the flickering light play over her face, glisten on her lips, shimmer in her eyes. Lovely and distant, she was so close he could touch her.

But Briny feared he might never reach her.

Chapter Five

"What did they do to you, girl?" Kneeling on the floor beside his decrepit old dog, Brindon shook Reba's head until her jowls flapped. She responded with a rumbling "Woof," her thick tail wagging slowly from side to side. He whispered a few more sweet nothings, and her long pink tongue lolled out and swiped his face.

Cringing at the moist show of canine devotion, Dorian folded her arms on her chest. "You have to admit she does smell better."

"Yeah, but I could live without the pink bows and matching toenail polish," he said. "Fluff and froufrou won't turn a bloodhound into a poodle. Look at her face, the poor old girl feels ridiculous." He tugged the stuck-on ribbons from the brown fur and patted the dog's flank. "She used to be in law enforcement, you know."

"You don't say?" Dorian eyed the nearly comatose animal skeptically.

"Old Reba was the top tracker in five counties." Brindon hugged the dog, more demonstrative with his pet than Dorian's mother had ever been with her only child. Dorian felt a momentary longing to be on the receiving end of so much affection, but such longings were best ignored.

"She lost her scent skills," he went on. "Could have been a virus. Since she was no good as a tracker, the sheriff's department was going to...put her down." He whispered to protect Reba's sensibilities.

"So how did you end up with her?"

"Sprung her out of lockup." He scratched the hound's head. "Right girl? Putting her to sleep didn't seem very grateful."

"You're very attached to her."

"We're attached to each other, all right. We've been together eight years. She's sixteen. One hundred and twelve in dog years. She doesn't have much time left and I want her to enjoy her old age."

"That's very kind of you." Brindon was sentimental; she wasn't. She'd never wanted a pet or the responsibility of another creature's happiness. For years, ensuring her own happiness had been her only goal. Maybe helping Brindon would give her a more worthy goal. "You really are a goodhearted guy, aren't you?"

"I know the difference between right and wrong," he demurred. "Putting Reba down would have been wrong. If you have some remover stuff, I'd like to clean this polish off her claws."

"Can't you wait until tomorrow?" Despite Reba's contribution to the criminal justice system, Dorian had her doubts about the holding capacity of the dog's ancient bladder. "Why don't you take her out for a short walk. She's been cooped up all day, I'm sure she needs to...go."

Brindon agreed, and after attaching a leash to the mutt's collar led Reba out into the hall. As soon as the elevator doors closed, Dorian darted around the apartment searching for odoriferous evidence of the dog's lapse in self-control. She sighed in relief when she found none. The carpet was as pristine as ever. One less thing to worry about.

By the time she'd changed into high-fashion sweats that had never seen the inside of a gym, her houseguests had returned.

Reba, exhausted from her strenuous stroll, collapsed in a sleepy pile on the floor. Since Brindon would be sharing her apartment for a while, Dorian gave him an overdue tour.

After making the circuit, she offered him his choice of bedrooms. To her everlasting relief, he chose the one farthest from hers. She had no intention of acting on the sensual impulses that had plagued her all day, but at least temptation would sleep on the opposite side of the large apartment.

After helping Brindon hang his new clothes in the walk-about closet, Dorian led him into the spacious kitchen. He found a place on the floor for the dog's water bowl and food dish. Talking to the mutt the whole time as if she were a child who understood everything he said, he poured Reba's dinner from a large sack of dog food he'd brought with him. He explained the special blend was formulated for delicate doggy stomachs.

He sat at the breakfast table and watched as Dorian opened a burlap bag of prized Jamaican coffee beans, measured them carefully into an electric mill and punched on the power.

"There's an easier way to make coffee, you know." He spoke over the grinder, his tone curious and helpful. "Have you ever tried instant? All you have to do is boil water."

"No, I never have." She smiled, dumped the fresh grounds into the basket and filled the coffeemaker with bottled water. "But thanks for the tip."

He shrugged, and his openly curious gaze took in the lighted shelf of carefully labeled spice jars and the gleaming copper-bottomed pots hanging from a rack suspended over the stove. Though she rarely cooked on the restaurant-size gas range, Dorian had ordered the model featured most often in her favorite decorating magazines. Her top-of-the-line refrigerator did everything but sing the blues, yet was mostly used to chill bottles of Evian.

Dorian owned three sets of dinnerware, formal, casual and everyday, and enough silver service and crystal stemware to outfit a battalion. She threw fabulous dinner parties, catered by the up-and-coming chef of the hour, yet she seldom ate a full meal.

"This is a cheery kitchen. Real homey." Brindon thanked her politely for the mug of hot coffee. "You must do a lot of cooking."

"Not really." At his questioning look, she added, "I don't have time." He didn't need to know her culinary skills had stalled out at the nuking-frozen-entrées-for-one level. Maybe she would be more interested in cooking if she had someone to appreciate her efforts. Someone with a zesty appetite who preferred home cooking over haute cuisine. Flipping through her mental Rolodex of friends, acquaintances and ex-lovers, she could not produce a single name who met that criterion.

Brindon would. However, he was neither friend nor lover. He was her employer. And while he lived in her home, she would not blur the line separating them. Her cooking skills were limited, but she *did* know mixing pleasure and business was a sure recipe for disaster.

"If you don't mind, I'd like to go over my plans for the next few days before we turn in." The evening had veered sharply toward pleasure, best get back to business.

"I'm ready to get down to hard work." He rubbed his hands together enthusiastically before taking a sip of coffee. "You know, this tastes *better* than instant."

"I'm glad you think so." She pulled a notebook from a drawer and sat down across the table from him. "The first thing we need to do is get you a new vehicle."

"Why?"

"Some of the tenants have complained about your truck. I promised we would get it off the street tomorrow." Her grandmother owned the building, and Dorian didn't want management contacting her.

"Why would people complain? It's not hurting anything."

"Appearances. Tenants pay a lot to live here. They don't want to look at a beat-up old pickup truck when they come home after a long day."

"I just spent big bucks fixing it up."

"Fixing it up?" she echoed. The thing looked like it had been through a twister.

"I put on new tires, installed a starter and clutch. Oil and lube job. My truck's running better than it has for months," he protested.

"Have you actually *looked* at your truck lately?"

He grimaced. "Yeah, maybe it is out of place here. I guess I could trade for a newer model."

"Actually, I think I should call a charity and have it towed away. If that's all right with you."

"What would they do with it?"

"I don't know. But it would go for a good cause, and we wouldn't have to deal with details. Would you prefer a Lamborghini or a Ferrari? I can make some calls, set up test-drives. How about tomorrow afternoon?"

"I want to buy American."

She looked up from her notebook. "American? Why?"

"To support the economy?"

"The U.S. economy will not crumble if you buy a foreign car, Brindon."

"Maybe not, but what if everybody did? Besides, I'm not the slick sports car type. How about I just get a new truck?"

She crossed out lines on her pad. "I don't think a truck is the way to go. A truck, even a new one, won't project the right image." She tapped the pen on the paper. "How about a luxury sports utility vehicle? They're as big as a truck, but more trendy."

"And a lot more expensive."

"You have plenty of money, you can afford to spend some on yourself." She hid her discomfort under a blanket of impatience. Their conversation unnerved her because in his gentle, unassuming way, Brindon constantly questioned her values. Or maybe he made her question them. Like a religion, those values filled up the empty places in her life, and she did not like having them put under a microscope. They would not stand up to close examination. He was paying her enough to be tolerant, but she found his stubborn lack of self-interest as exasperating as her attraction to him. "Consider a new vehicle an investment.

"Okay," he agreed reluctantly. "Just so long as it's made in America."

They discussed option preferences, and she made a note to call area dealers to bring vehicles by for Brindon's approval. Once the car question was settled, she moved on. "We'll stop by the bookstore in the morning and pick out your textbooks. For starters, we need to get volumes on music, art, travel, food and wine, along with a few fiction classics. This is a list from one of my old college literature classes." She slid the sheet of paper across the table. "Have you read any of these books?"

He skimmed down the list and shook his head. "No, but I want to make up for the time I've wasted. My teachers always said I had the smarts but I didn't have the focus. I'm focused now."

"Good. You'll be a quick study." Pretending to write, she watched him and speculated on the kind of life he must have had. He'd been a little boy when he lost his mother, and his father hadn't cared. Dorian knew all too well what being alone felt like. At least Cassandra had tried to substitute material things for love. Brindon hadn't even had that.

He'd spent his formative years in an institution with abandoned, troubled boys. Dorian had spent hers in an institution with abandoned, rich girls. Except for the quality of the food and extracurricular activities, the two were not all that different.

"I'd like to learn about economics and finance," he said. "And how to use a computer."

"Not a problem. I'll order a PC and get you the tech support you need. I can't help you with the other, but I'll find someone who can." Obviously, if she were a financial wizard, she wouldn't have gotten herself into this mess.

But if she hadn't, she never would have met Brindon. Dorian's stomach fluttered. Given their very separate lives, the fact their paths had crossed at all was almost a miracle. She'd thought Granny Pru had slammed a door in her face. But by forcing responsibility on her, her grandmother had opened a window of opportunity.

Because Dorian had been shipped off to boarding school at an early age, only in the past four years had she spent quality time with her grandmother. Cassandra's jealous, spiteful nature had denied them the kind of relationship Dorian longed for. One more reason to resent her mother. Prudence Burrell was the only stable force in her only heir's life, and Dorian hated to let her down. Maybe she could yet redeem herself in her grandmother's eyes.

"Do you think Malcolm would be willing to teach me about the stock market and how to handle investments?" Brindon's question drew Dorian back into the conversation.

"I'm sure he will, so long as he doesn't have to give away trade secrets."

"I think financial management is something I need to know. I have to learn how to make my money work for me."

"Yes." He was right, of course. She'd never thought about money, beyond what it could buy. Odd how *not* having funds made her appreciate what she had. Maybe sitting in on Malcolm's lessons would be helpful. She could learn how to make *her* money work. She scribbled another note.

"Anything else?" he asked.

"Oh, I'm planning to bring in a voice coach for you." Schmoozing fellow Art Leaguers had netted a friend of a friend of a friend who handled staff development for a local corporation. When she called, the man had graciously recommended a specialist in dialect reduction.

"Voice coach? Do I have to take singing lessons, too?" His crooked grin sent a wavelet of pleasure coursing through Dorian. Looking at a man had never been so much fun. The changing expressions playing across Brindon's animated face were as entertaining as a slide show.

"No. But we need to work on your speech." She explained the inverse relationship between accent and perceived intelligence.

"So you're saying people will think better of me if I sound more like Dan Rather and less like Gomer Pyle?"

"It's a sad fact but true. Learning to speak properly isn't hard. It's all in the vowels." She had quashed her own Texas intonation by the end of her first term at Creighton by mimicking her Boston roommate. A professional would teach Brindon correctly.

"Whatever you say. I've placed myself in your hands, so I trust you to do the right thing."

Dorian swallowed hard. Didn't he realize how dangerous such confidence could be? He was so accepting and she was so...unreliable in caring for others.

"You wouldn't happen to have any snacks, would you?" His brows lifted apologetically. "I'm getting hungry again."

"After the huge meal we had tonight?" She'd eaten with rare gusto, as though Brindon's healthy hunger had liberated her, making her own seem more acceptable.

His blue gaze captured hers. "I'm one of those people who is always hungry. After Mom died, there never seemed to be any food in the house. My old man wasn't around much."

"Your father left you alone?"

"Sometimes." He shrugged. "Maybe it's because I missed so many meals when I was a kid, but I never seem to get enough. Takes a lot to satisfy me."

"Really?" She reminded herself he was talking about food. Mr. Earnest was not the double-entendre type.

"Fortunately, I never gain weight, no matter how much I eat. My cottage mother back at Los Huerfanos told me I had the metabolism of an adolescent wolverine."

"Lucky you." She shoved away from the table and his curious gaze. Searching the pantry she found a half-empty bag of peanut butter rice cakes. "This is all the snack food I have until I go to the market. Sorry."

Brindon bit into a rice cake, smiling and nodding as he chewed. And chewed. Dorian realized the expiration date had probably passed. He took a big gulp of coffee and closed the bag, which he slid back across the table. "I believe one will do me."

"You didn't like the rice cake?" She knew full well only good manners and willpower had enabled him to force down the unfamiliar, unsavory food.

"It was...okay. Peanut butter is one of my favorite flavors.'' He glanced at the bag as if unsure what he had just swallowed.

"But you said you were hungry.'' She extended the bag. She shouldn't tease him, but she couldn't resist. He was so determined to be polite. "Are you sure you don't want another one?''

"I'll wait for breakfast. One of those things will last a man a lifetime.''

She hid her grin by replacing the bag in the cabinet. So he was a one-rice-cake-in-a-lifetime kind of guy? Knowing bland, tasteless food did not appeal to Brindon's hearty appetite made acute physical awareness prick her like a knife. Did he believe in one woman for a lifetime as well? Dare she assume his sexual tastes were equally earthy and ravenous?

She'd received no complaints about her own performance skills, yet niggling doubt made her wonder if this direct and unsophisticated man would find her restraint and self-control as unappealing as low-cal food? His hunger had inspired her own tonight, for she had never enjoyed a meal as much as the dinner they had shared. And never had she succumbed to day-dreams as prurient as the ones dancing in and out of her consciousness all day.

Ordinarily she held back, prudently denying her craving for intimacy as she denied her craving for food, since wanting and hurting were fruit of the same tree. She'd hidden her emotional needs since an early age, but tonight she'd had a taste of something new and delicious.

Could this unlikely man be the one with whom she would no longer have to pretend?

The next morning, Briny took his hostess-tutor's advice and made himself at home. He suspected she might not be an early riser so he fed and watered Reba and took her out for a long walk, hoping Dorian would be up by the time he returned. She wasn't. He shaved and showered, then dressed in one of the new outfits she'd picked out. Still not a peep from her room. He chewed gum and watched CNN until the news anchor started repeating herself.

Nothing. He glanced at Dorian's closed door. Eight o'clock. She was a rich heiress unaccustomed to getting up for work, so she probably slept in. Finally he couldn't stand waiting any longer. With his stomach growling like a grizzly in springtime, he wandered into her magazine-pretty kitchen to scare up some breakfast. After peeking inside the whitewashed cabinets, he knew exactly how Old Mother Hubbard must have felt.

Except for a few staples, the cupboards were bare.

No problem. Briny had known plenty of lean years and was an old hand at making do. He whistled tunelessly as he assembled his breakfast, then carried the bowl to what Dorian called the morning room. Her apartment had surprised him almost as much as she had. Based on the I-couldn't-care-less attitude she hid behind, he expected her home to be as sleek, glamorous and modern as the clothes she wore. Instead, the place was filled with feminine frills and flowers and old-fashioned charm. Maybe her home projected the woman she wanted to be, instead of the one she tried to tell the world she was.

Sitting at the table in a bright pool of sunlight, Briny admired the glittering Dallas skyline. Today was the kind of perfect, cloudless day that made a man glad just to be alive. He grinned, knowing he'd be happy if the sky suddenly went black and started throwing down lightning bolts.

He had a whole new day to spend with Dorian.

He was still eating when she padded in, half-asleep and as crabby as an old cat. Her hair was caught up in a cockeyed ponytail, and she was wearing her sweet Dori face, devoid of makeup, the way he liked to see her. Instead of the sexy little satin number she'd worn before, she was dressed in a long, thick, old-lady robe. She poured last night's coffee into a mug which she placed in the microwave oven before offering a mumbled "good morning."

"It's a fine day for the race." He didn't try to temper his enthusiasm.

"What race?" she mumbled.

"The human race."

She groaned, then stifled a yawn as the mug turned around on the carousel. "Been up long?"

"Not very."

"Liar."

"Early bird gets the worm," he reminded.

"Worms are highly overrated."

"Are you hungry?" he asked. "I can make you some breakfast."

She peered into the bowl in front of him, and her nose wrinkled in distaste. "What in the name of all that is holy are you eating?"

"Peanut butter with maple syrup and sugar. I hope you don't mind. You said to make myself at home."

"I didn't say make yourself sick."

He spooned up a big bite which he held out. "Try some. It doesn't taste as bad as it looks."

"Nothing could possibly taste as bad as that looks. But no, thank you. I'll stick to reheated coffee."

He shrugged and took another bite.

"You do know how disgusting that stuff is, right?"

He nodded, unable to clear his mouth enough to speak.

"Good. Just checking." The microwave dinged and she removed the mug.

"Don't be a food snob." He took a gulp of orange juice. "Back in Slapdown, there were times when this was all I had. Fills you up and packs a lot of calories. A man can work all morning on a bowl of peanut butter and syrup." He took another bite.

"This isn't Slapdown," she reminded again. "And you're not Tom Joad. We'll go to the supermarket and stock up on things that are actually edible."

He chewed for a few seconds to clear the sticky peanut butter concoction before speaking. "Tom who?"

"Joad. A character in *The Grapes of Wrath*." She took a sip of the now-bitter brew and grimaced.

He should have figured out how to work the fancy coffee mill and made her a fresh pot. He couldn't think straight around her. "I saw that movie." Finally, something he knew about. He'd watched the film several times on the late show. "Henry Fonda, right?"

"Right. But it's also a novel by John Steinbeck. I think it's on your reading list." She glanced again at his bowl of syrup-topped peanut butter and shuddered. Covering her eyes with her hand, she took her coffee and headed for her room.

"What's wrong?" he asked.

"I can't watch you eat that," she called over her shoulder. "As soon as I get dressed, we'll go to the bookstore, then the supermarket. I'll make some calls, and by the time we get back, there'll be some new wheels here for you to try out."

"Whatever you say. You're the boss." Peanut butter swimming in syrup might make carrying on a conversation difficult—he had enough manners not to talk with his mouth full—but his gooey breakfast really wasn't any more disgusting than béarnaise sauce.

At five o'clock, Dorian checked her to-do list. They had accomplished all the day's chores except one. Brindon's ratty old truck was still parked on the street. They'd been so busy at the bookstore and with the test-drives, she had not found time to call and have the thing hauled away. She was even more eager to get rid of the pile of junk recently replaced in Brindon's affections by a gleaming black Lincoln Navigator.

She tried calling a nonprofit organization she knew took vehicular contributions, but they were already closed for the day. "We didn't get rid of the truck," she told Brindon as she hung up the phone. "Snarky Mrs. Cortina will report me to the tenant's organization again."

Brindon laid aside the thick art book he'd been studying. "Let's go."

"Where?"

"To get rid of the truck."

They drove around for half an hour before he found what he was looking for. He pulled past a bus stop and parked at the curb. "Come on."

Dorian had no idea what he was up to. She'd asked, but all he would say was, "You'll see." She followed him as he approached a tired-looking woman seated on the bus stop bench with three lively little boys.

"Excuse me, ma'am. May I ask you something?" His polite approach seemed to put the woman at ease.

"If you're going to ask me to have your children, I'm not interested. Don't have the time or the energy." She gave him a weary, yet appreciative look.

He blushed. "I was wondering if you have a vehicle."

"Sure. My Cadillac is in the shop." She wore a pink waitress uniform with the name Sue embroidered over the pocket. The dress was stained and frayed around the edges.

"We don't have a Cadiwac, Mommy." The oldest of her three sons appeared to be about five years old.

"I was thinking…may I?" Dressed in a crisp blue shirt and impeccably pressed khaki slacks, Brindon indicated the bench, and the woman slid over to make room for him. She held a squirming toddler on her lap. Dorian stood a couple of feet away and watched the exchange. Even though the mother and Brindon were about the same age, Sue had obviously taken a few more laps around the track. She looked as worn-out as her uniform.

"I'll bet riding the bus with this crew can be a trial." His soft words weren't critical or judging, just observant.

"Oh, it's a picnic. I gotta work all day, then ride the bus to the sitter and catch another one home. It's never on time. Mornings, I have to make connections in reverse, which gives me plenty of chances to be late. When that happens, the boss chews me out and docks my pay. If I'm short I can't pay my rent."

"And mean old Mr. Hagger yells at Mama," the biggest boy put in helpfully.

"He's my landlord," she explained.

"Do you have a husband?" Brindon asked.

"Not anymore. You want the job?"

"Thank you for the offer, ma'am, but no. Don't worry, you'll find the right man. We all have a right person out there somewhere. Waiting to find us."

"You believe that?"

"Yes, I do."

"I wish Prince Charming would get the lead out then," she said with a derisive chuckle. "The clock's a'tickin'."

"See that truck over there?" Brindon pointed.

"Yeah?"

"I know it doesn't look like much, but the engine runs good, the tires are new, and the gas tank is full. I'd like you to have it."

Cadiwac boy jumped up and down, inciting his siblings, but his mother's eyes narrowed. "Why?"

"Because you need transportation." He removed a folded paper from his shirt pocket.

"What's the catch?" The woman shushed her exuberant children and looked around as if expecting to find a hidden TV camera. "There's gotta be a catch. People don't give away trucks."

"No catch. Here's the title." His smile was brilliant with sincerity, and the wary woman relaxed into acceptance. "Dorian, do you have a pen so I can transfer the paperwork to this lady?"

Dorian unzipped her organizer and handed him a gold pen costing more than the woman probably made in a day, including tips. He asked her full name, then carefully signed over ownership of the truck he'd driven from Slapdown.

Sue, tired waitress and frazzled mother of three, sat there, fat tears welling in her eyes. "I've been praying for something good to finally happen to me. This is like a wish come true."

"It's just an old truck." He dismissed his generosity. "But maybe it'll ease some of your troubles." Brindon handed her the title and pulled a wad of bills from his wallet. "You need to buy insurance and safety seats for your children." He ruffled the baby's downy hair. "Promise me now, no matter how much you might want to, you won't spend this on anything else. You have to keep this cargo safe."

"I will. Thank you, sir." She stuffed the money and title into her battered purse. "I can't believe you're doing this."

"Done deal," he said with a chuckle. "Here." He took her hand and placed the key in her palm, folding her fingers over with a squeeze. He leaned in and spoke so quietly Dorian had to strain to hear him. "You're doing a good job, Sue. I can tell you love these little men of yours. Don't ever stop."

"What's your name?" The mother swiped tears with the back of her hand. "I need to know who my fairy godfather is."

"Just call me Briny." He carried the middle boy and helped Sue stow her brood in the cab of their new truck. The boys waved noisy goodbyes, and he and Dorian stood on the curb and watched them drive away.

She dashed the dampness from her own eyes before he caught her being sentimental. How many charity fund-raisers had she attended in her lifetime? How many worthwhile foundations had she supported? She'd written checks for so many deserving causes, she'd lost track. Yet she had never felt as good about giving as she did at this moment.

"You're amazing," she said in quiet awe.

"No, I'm not. But I *am* hungry."

She looked around. They were a long way from home. "While you were caught up in good-deed doing, did you consider how we're going to get back to the West End?" She reached for her cell phone to call a taxi, but he had other ideas.

"Yup." He took her hand and led her toward the recently vacated bench. "We're gonna catch a bus."

Chapter Six

Brindon's intellect took shape under Dorian's tutelage the way a rough-cut gem finds its fire in the hands of a skilled diamond cutter. A conscientious student, he learned quickly, exceeding her expectations. He devoured new experiences with lavish appetite, and the more he accomplished, the more she was inspired to challenge him.

Watching Brindon's world open up through lessons she planned, conducted or arranged, recalled to Dorian her adolescent ambition to teach. As a lonely, idealistic boarding school student, tutoring a man like Brindon wasn't what she'd had in mind. That didn't make her present duties less satisfying. For the first time in her life, she knew the joy of purpose. And how good having purpose could feel.

The more time she spent with Brindon, the more important he became to her. Determined to hide her burgeoning emotions from his patient scrutiny, Dorian waved her new laser pointer like a magic wand, spinning the next few weeks into a blur of activity. Concentrating on work made resisting the heady pull of inappropriate desire less nerve-racking and pushed her pupil closer to his goals.

Despite her resolve to conduct herself professionally, there

were times when Dorian dared to hope Brindon shared her
feelings: when their heads bent closely over a book and his
sweet, cinnamon-flavored breath mingled with hers; when
their bodies brushed in passing and the imagined thrum of his
heart set hers racing; when she caught him watching her with
a serious expression, but looked away quickly when their
gazes met; when he would start to speak, stop short, go
strangely quiet.

But surely that was wishful thinking on her part, for in all
the hours they spent in close company, his behavior never
breached the walls of propriety. She was more disappointed
than she cared to admit even to herself, but Brindon did not
treat her as an object of desire.

Why should he? What would a kind, generous, hardworking
man see in a spoiled heiress whose biggest decisions to date
involved lunching and shopping? He'd been clear from the
start. He didn't want to be ''a rich loafer who lived fluffy,
with no thought for anyone else.'' Unfortunately, the phrase
described Dorian and everyone she knew.

Her friends, recently returned from a Cozumel beach resort,
were curious, and clamored to meet her new ''project.'' Hes-
itant to introduce Brindon to them, she told herself she wanted
to protect him from their cynicism and empty extravagance.
But what if she really wanted to keep him to herself? Worse
still, what if she just wanted him?

Not what he could buy, or what he might become when his
education was complete. Him. For what he was now. A beautiful spirit in a beautiful body. Wrestling with her conscience
was new to Dorian, but she was smart enough to realize the
most self-serving act of her self-serving life would be give in
to her crazy, needy urges. Especially since he had not indicated he wanted more from her than introduction into society.

Brindon was a man of principle, waiting patiently for one
right woman to come along so they could live happily ever
after. She was not that woman. She didn't believe in fairy tales
or true love. She might not have a head for business, but she
knew trading Brindon's trust for a few hours of physical pleasure would be no bargain.

At present she could see only one meaningful way to fit into his life. She had to earn his respect, be the best tutor his money could buy. Their budding friendship was the most genuine alliance she'd ever formed. Maybe in the process of proving herself to him, she would prove something to herself.

A physical relationship was doomed to end. They always did. But if she could learn to be a friend to him...maybe he would stay a little longer. At least until he embarked upon the new life for which she was helping him prepare. She'd been empty inside before he'd swept into her life, and when he left, she would be emptier still.

Dorian dealt with the problem the only way she knew how. She kept Brindon busy with study and struggled to deny the strange and tender feelings taking root in her heart.

One by one, Brindon read the books on the list she'd provided, soaking up the words like a thirsty garden soaks up a summer shower. During their frequent lively discussions, he made insightful observations and surprised Dorian by counting Jane Austen's work among his favorites. Further proof he was a sucker for happy endings. She had no doubt he would get one. She did not think she would.

With the help of a young computer ace named Justin, Brindon mastered the equipment set up in an extra bedroom. Before long he was an avid Web surfer, and spent hours researching the numerous charitable foundations courting his patronage. Determined to use his money for the greater good, Brindon refused to be pressured into making major monetary decisions until he could do so with confidence.

To that end he met twice weekly with Malcolm O'Neal for one-on-one sessions. Deciding that learning a thing or two wouldn't hurt her, Dorian accompanied Brindon and took notes as the financial planner explained the ins and outs of money management. Not in-depth enough to make his services unnecessary, she noted cynically, but enough to make Brindon a more savvy consumer of those services.

One day during Malcolm's discussion of estate planning, Dorian was struck by the fact that as powerful as Granny Pru was, she would not live forever. As the only grandchild, Dorian stood to inherit Chaco Oil, if the elderly woman didn't get fed up enough to cut her out of the will first. What a sobering thought for a woman who could barely run her own life, much less a Fortune 500 corporation. Accepting her grandmother's mortality and the inevitability of her future, Dorian vowed to become a worthy successor to the kingdom founded on her great-grandfather's lucky oil strike.

She hadn't accomplished much in her twenty-six years, but maybe it wasn't too late. She might yet shoulder her obligations and earn her grandmother's trust. Before Brindon, Dorian had been on the fast track to nowhere, following in her mother's idle footsteps, drifting from one pointless social event to another. But watching a man abandoned as a child and voted Most Likely To Serve Time take charge of his destiny gave her the courage to take charge of her own.

During the first month of their arrangement, they didn't go out much.

In the evenings, Dorian helped Brindon with his "homework." They pored over *Investor's Daily* and researched the stocks Malcolm assigned them to investigate. By gaining knowledge and accepting possibilities, Brindon's unexpected riches became less burden and more blessing. Through their studies, Dorian learned something he had apparently understood all along. Wealth gave power and demanded responsibility.

Knowledge determined whether wealth was used as an implement of success or an instrument of destruction.

On the cultural front, the computer guru helped Dorian use her art history education to create a self-guiding computer program by scanning photographs of famous masterpieces and keying in brief descriptions. Brindon studied his way through the ages, learning to recognize and name classic objets d'art while gaining a basic knowledge of the works' histories and the artists who'd created them.

They spent long, quiet hours in her apartment, reading and listening to classical music CDs. Dorian knew her saturation strategy had paid off when Brindon could beat her at her own "name that tune" game.

Proclaiming turnabout was fair play, the student also became the teacher. Quickly tiring of restaurant meals, Brindon
insisted he and Dorian take private cooking lessons from a
sous chef employed by her favorite caterer. Brindon's tastes
were simple and veered toward the robust, but he was adven-
turous and accustomed to fending for himself in the kitchen.
To Dorian's never-ending dismay, he soon tempted her self-
control with spicy pots of roadhouse chili and savory cuts of
meat barbecued on the range-top grill.

She didn't acquire cooking skills as quickly as Brindon and
was less of a risk taker, but eventually she learned enough to
hold her own with dishes like angel-hair pasta and rosemary
baked chicken. Playing dueling saucepans, they engaged in
friendly competition to see whose meals were the most enticing.

One day in late July they finished the chicken quesadillas
Brindon had whipped up for lunch. He asked an unexpected
question. "What can you tell me about The Children's Development Fund?"

Dorian looked up in surprise. "What do you want to
know?"

"They've asked me for a donation, and I just wondered
what they do with their money."

"They do good…things. That's what charities are. Organizations that do good things."

"I don't understand," he said wryly. "Can you vague that
up for me?"

"Didn't you receive a brochure outlining fund allocations
with the donation request?"

"Yes, I read the brochure. But 'providing recreational, cultural and educational activities for underprivileged children'
doesn't tell me much."

She shrugged and carried their empty plates to the dishwasher. They had a deal; whoever cooked was exempt from
cleanup duty. "If it's important to you, I can make some calls.
Maybe I can find out."

"But you said you give this organization a sizable annual
donation."

"Yes, I do. They have a wonderful theme ball every October. Last year they threw a safari gala, and brought in the crocodile guy from TV. They had the most amazing decorations. An appropriate gift assures seating at a good table up front."

His forehead furrowed in confusion. "You give them money so you can go to their party?"

His oversimplification made her uncomfortable. "No. Of course not. The Children's Development Fund is a worthy cause. The party is a perk and raises a lot of money."

"How do you know it's a worthy cause?"

"Because it is," she said lamely. Her apprentice do-gooder had an infuriating habit of zeroing in on her inadequacies. She tried to do her part in the philanthropy sector, but her primary role was as a highly sought-after guest. Any fund-raising event attended by a Burrell was guaranteed print space in the social pages.

"Haven't you ever wanted to see your money in action?"

What a strange question. "Why would I want that?" Every year, her budget included a fairly large sum for donation to charities of her choice, and she felt darned good about her generosity. Asking what the organizations did with the checks they cashed seemed presumptuous.

"Make the call," he said with conviction. "Tell them we want a tour of whatever project receives the largest allocation of funds."

"We do?" She closed the dishwasher and punched the on button. "A tour?"

"And tell them we don't want some slick-talking public relations type showing us around. Ask for the director."

She let out a slow breath. "That might be a little difficult."

"Why?" he asked reasonably. "I would think a reputable charity would be ready and willing to put their mouths where they want our money to be."

She couldn't argue with his logic, even if not questioning where her donated dollars went made her feel inadequate. "I'll see what I can do."

* * *

The next day Marjorie Treadwell, director of The Children's Development Fund escorted Brindon and Dorian through three women's and two homeless shelters where CDF sponsored a program called Kid-Time for children in the system. They observed music lessons, art classes and a roomful of tumbling tots on floor mats. Arriving at the last stop on the tour in time for story hour, they were invited to sit on colorful carpet squares with a squirming group of preschoolers.

When a tiny boy asked to sit in Brindon's lap, he was welcomed with a heartfelt "sure thing, pardner" which showed a careless disregard for his eleven-hundred-dollar Hugo Boss suit. A red-haired pixy with a pacifier plugged in her mouth snuggled up to Mrs. Treadwell. However, not one child found Dorian's lap inviting. Not that she wanted them leaking on her jade raw-silk coat dress.

During snack break, several youngsters vied for Brindon's attention. To her surprise he refilled their cups and wiped their spills with a good-natured humor that made Mary Poppins look like a grouch.

Feeling as invisible and about as welcome as a plague-carrying virus, Dorian stood apart from Brindon and his shrieking fan club. Did she emit, like those mole deterrents people stuck in their yards, some kind of high-frequency signal that repelled animals and small children? Maybe she would have seemed more sociable had she accepted the stupid graham cracker and apple juice when the trays were passed.

Later Mrs. Treadwell drove them back to the CDF office and offered to answer any questions they might have. Brindon removed a legal pad from the new briefcase Dorian had chosen for him and read from a list he'd prepared in advance. "How many employees on your payroll, ma'am?"

The director, a kind-eyed woman in her sixties, was also prepared. "We have three full-time employees who run the office and administer our funds. Two additional workers are hired for three months a year to plan and oversee our annual fund-raiser. Program leaders are volunteers, some local corporate employees wishing to do community service. Others are interns from university education classes fulfilling clinical requirements by working in our program.''

Brindon nodded. ''What percentage of CDF's annual income is spent directly on programs for the children, and how much goes to overhead and administrative costs?''

Dorian was impressed by Brindon's questions. As with everything he did, he'd put a lot of thought into them. She also admired the careful diction he used these days. Not only had his pronunciation improved over the past few weeks, so had his grammar and vocabulary. The dialect coach had turned out to be a regular slave driver, making him practice until the corn had been distilled into a smooth, mellow, whiskey-voiced baritone.

''We budget twenty-five percent for administrative expenses.'' Mrs. Treadwell gave him a wry look. ''When I mentioned we have three full-time employees, I didn't mean to imply any of us are well paid.''

He grinned. ''And putting on the ball every year must cost a lot.''

''Private benefactors sponsor the gala. Without the money it raises, we would have to cut back on the services we offer.''

He made another note. ''Mrs. Treadwell, tell me something. If you could have your fondest wish for CDF granted, what would your wish be?''

''Seriously?'' When he nodded, she went on in a rush. ''I'd love to place computers with educational software in all the centers, but unfortunately, there are more pressing and survival-related needs. Some of the youngsters come from homes torn apart by domestic violence. Others haven't even had homes for months. As a result they miss a lot of school. Computers would enable them to catch up and maintain their level of education while they're in transition to a better life.''

She glanced at Brindon and smiled. ''That's my wish. But it's just a pipe dream at present.''

When they arrived back at the office, Brindon shook the director's hand and thanked her for showing them around.

''So, Mr. Tucker,'' she said with a hopeful look, ''can we expect to seat you at the head table next fall?''

Dorian recognized the woman's cautiously phrased request. Only the most generous patrons were offered those coveted seats.

Brindon spoke, and Dorian feared he'd misunderstood the director's question. "I don't think so, Mrs. Treadwell. I'm not much of a partygoer."

The woman's face fell in undisguised disappointment, but she extended her hand graciously. "I understand. Thank you for your time. I hope you will keep us in mind for next year."

"I may not be a partygoer," he said as he took out his checkbook. "But I believe in what you're trying to do." He wrote out a check. "I've priced computers recently. This should cover five PCs for each shelter, plus a couple thousand for software. You strike me as a shrewd negotiator, ma'am. Maybe you can get more for your money. I want the kids to have computers, so please earmark the funds for that purpose."

The director, an obviously battle-hardened veteran of the charity wars, blanched when she saw the amount. She accepted the check with a shaky hand. "I don't know what to say. Thank you."

"No need to say anything." Brindon smiled and said goodbye. He turned to leave, then seemed to remember an important detail. "I do need a receipt for Uncle Sam though, if you don't mind."

Warmed by Brindon's generosity, Dorian couldn't help smiling when she recognized Malcolm's obvious influence. Brindon had learned a lot about handling money during the past few weeks. But he was teaching her about the spirit of giving.

"I still don't think golf is something I want to get mixed up in." Briny had been dead set against the idea since Dorian first suggested he join her ritzy country club. She'd ignored his protests. She insisted belonging to the right club was critical to his social standing and acceptance into the right circles. By name dropping and string pulling, Dorian had gotten his membership application rushed through the approval process.

Though he carried the embossed card in his wallet, he wasn't fool enough to believe he would ever really belong.

"Oh, for Pete's sake," she said as he turned his new SUV into the long, graceful drive. "It's golf, not organized crime."

"I already feel out of place." So far they'd kept close to her apartment. They had brought the outside world in, creating a cocoon of security for his explorations. Leaping out into the rarefied atmosphere of Rich World and walking among an alien race was a big step.

"You'll be fine."

"I've never been on a golf course before. I don't even know anyone who has." He pulled up in front of the clubhouse as Dorian directed, got out and handed the Navigator's key to the valet. He was about to remove the golf bags from the back when an eager caddy ran up. The poor kid was eight inches shorter and a good seventy pounds lighter, and Briny felt strange standing by watching him do all the work. But evidently the wealthier a man was, the less he was expected to lift and tote. Then he had to spend time in the gym, exercising muscles weakened from lack of use. Made about as much sense as a boreh heat scrub.

"You're going to love golf. Wait and see."

"Seems like a damned silly game to me," he muttered. He wasn't the same clueless rube he'd been a month ago, but he wasn't ready to go public. He and Dorian had finally found some tentative common ground, and he was beginning to climb the glass hill. Maybe, like the farmer's son in the fairy tale his mother had read to him, he would someday succeed in reaching the lonely princess and win her heart.

The unbidden thought hit him in the face like a blast from a cold shower. Could he really win her heart? In the beginning he hadn't thought he had a snowflake's chance with her. What had happened the last few weeks to give him hope? When had he started thinking he might be good enough for a woman like Dorian Burrell?

Did he want to pursue a relationship with her when his tutoring was over? Yes. He realized now that he did. He wanted a chance to find out if Dorian might be the woman he'd always dreamed about.

But if he made a fool of himself in front of her snooty country club friends, he'd slide down the slippery slope of the glass hill and lose what little progress he'd made. If she was reminded of how different they really were, her cool eyes might start viewing him as a project again.

He wanted her to see him as a man.

"Golf is more than a game." She'd brought her pink bag of high-dollar clubs and planned to play nine holes with her friend while he had his first lesson. "It's a metaphor for life. Important contacts are made on the greens, historic deals closed on the back nine. All true gentlemen play golf."

"Maybe I should graduate gentleman school before I try this."

"I'm the teacher, and playing a passable game of golf is one of your graduation requirements. You've joined the club, and I've arranged the lessons. Stop grousing and enjoy them."

Inside the elaborately carved doors, the clubhouse decor screamed "money" at the top of its oak-paneled lungs. No wonder joining cost a cool forty thousand. Luxury did not come cheap. Briny eyed the well-groomed club members togged out in expensive sportswear. They belonged here. He did not. Bridging the gap would take more than the right outfit and a hundred-dollar haircut.

Uneasiness settled in his gut like a bad burrito, yet Briny smiled as he matched his pace to Dorian's. Only a woman with her inborn sense of style could look elegant in golf shorts and a visor. Sexy, too. The long, tanned perfection of her legs made his mouth go dry. "We'll be finished in time for lunch, right?"

She handed him over to the golf pro with a long-suffering moan. "Barring the rice cake incident, have I ever allowed you to go hungry?"

He sighed. *Every day, darlin'.* He was consumed with hunger every time he caught the scent of her elusive perfume. Or heard her wind-chime laughter or accidentally touched her too-soft skin. Every day. With every breath he took.

Mesmerized by the hypnotic motion of her hips, he watched her stride down the wide corridor and disappear into the ladies' locker room. He fought an urge to follow her, back her up against the wall and kiss her senseless.

Lord, he had to find his own place. Soon. Being a gentleman was getting to be too much of a burden. Living with Dorian while maintaining a hands-off policy was CIA-quality torture. Briny didn't know how much longer he could tough it out. Or how many more cold showers he could take.

He felt like a starving man spread-eagled and staked out on a buffet table.

"You man miser, you. I can't believe you've been keeping this guy to yourself." Tiggy pulled clean clothes from the locker bearing her name on an engraved plaque. "You are a selfish, selfish girl."

"It's not like he's my personal love slave." Dorian waved a blow dryer over her damp hair, which accounted for the heat rushing to her face. They had run into Brindon and the pro behind the clubhouse after his lesson, and Tiggy had not shut up about him since. "He's my employer, and we have been very busy the past few weeks."

"I'll bet you have. In a tribute to *My Fair Lady*, our friends are calling you Henrietta Higgins to his Ebenezer Doolittle. I assumed he was some scruffy cowboy, fresh off the turnip truck." Tiggy tossed her towel aside, her all-over tan proof of the hours she'd logged on the nude beach during her vacation. She slipped into lacy French underwear, then wiggled into tight white Capri pants and a red off-the-shoulder cotton top before stepping into leather mules. "Boy, was I wrong. He's really hot."

Dorian fluffed her hair and pulled on a summery apricot sheath, then matching sandals. How could anyone describe Brindon with an overused word like *hot*? Such a description revealed nothing about him, didn't even sum up his physical appearance. It was superficial, like Tiggy.

"Our relationship is strictly professional." Keeping it that way was the only "right" thing Dorian had ever done.

The brunette paused in her lip gloss application. "Would you tell if it weren't?"

Dorian rolled her eyes. Had her friend always gotten on her nerves like this? "No. Because my working relationship is none of your business."

"You're a noble being. But then you always did exercise too much self-control with men. I'd be tempted to find out if that long, tall Texan looks half as good out of those clothes as he does in them."

"He's my boss. I don't think of him that way." Liar! Her conscience nearly choked on the blatant falsehood. How many nights had she lain awake in her empty bed, tormented by unwanted images of herself sprawled atop Brindon's big naked body? Beneath it? Beside it? Performing pretzel tricks on satin sheets? She'd had to run a slide show of Flemish paintings through her head in order to fall asleep.

"Well, he's not my boss." Tiggy's comment was flippant and lascivious. "And fortunately I have no such inhibitions. Judging by the number of women who drooled as he walked through the clubhouse, I'd say most of the female population is equally unprincipled. Better watch out, teacher. I would hate for you to get trampled in the stampede."

Tiggy's prediction that women would find Brindon as irresistible as he'd been to the tots at the shelter, but for a less wholesome reason, filled Dorian with sick dismay. They entered the dining room to meet him for lunch, but how could she eat with her stomach performing a complicated gymnastics routine? What was the matter with her? She had no claim on Brindon Tucker. He was a grown man. A free agent. A gorgeous ship with a sexy keel taking a little longer than normal to pass through her night.

So why did the thought of Tiggy following through on her threat to peel him out of his clothes make Dorian want to scratch her best friend's eyes out? She took a calming breath and fought the powerful impulse to drag him home and lock him in her penthouse apartment like a gender-bending Rapunzel, to prevent evil women from taking advantage of him.

Brindon stood when they entered the room, a relieved

where-have-you-been grin on his face. His dark hair was still damp from his shower, and he had changed from his golf clothes into casual olive trousers and a white cotton polo shirt with the club logo over the left breast. He looked perfect, to the manor born.

During the day, the club was filled with the very rich. The men all wore shirts flaunting logos of the exclusive courses they'd played. This was Brindon's first time at the country club, yet he blended into the room of rich, bored sophisticates like a peacock in an exotic aviary. Dorian had accomplished what she'd set out to do. Isn't that what she wanted? What she'd been paid to do?

Why, then, did she feel so awful?

"Mmm," Tiggy muttered under her breath as they approached the table. "I am *so* glad Mr. Long Tall is not my boss. But I'm even happier not to be burdened by nasty old scruples."

Which was why women like Tiggy and her friends did not stand a chance with Brindon. He possessed abundant scruples, and he deserved a woman with the same bone-deep integrity. Somewhere in the world was the woman meant for him.

Weighed down by sadness at the thought she wasn't the one, Dorian sank onto the chair Brindon held for her. Why was she suddenly so sad? Why did she feel as if she'd been shocked by a live wire and left limp and totally defenseless? There was one possibility she hadn't wanted to consider.

Dorian looked across the table at the wonderful man with whom she'd spent nearly every waking moment for the past month. She had a horrible suspicion about what was wrong. Why she felt so bad.

Dammit. She was in love.

Chapter Seven

Briny spotted Dorian and her friend as they entered the country club's gold and burgundy dining room. The tall, tanned brunette was a sultry head turner in tight pants and a form-fitting blouse, but his gaze didn't linger on her. He homed in on Dorian like a sub-seeking missile, and the sight of her filled him with relief and anticipation.

He'd been adrift since she had marooned him with the golf pro on the driving range this morning. Tense and unsure of his bearings, he'd floated around the elegant club, waiting to rejoin her. Now he could sit back and relax. Dorian was here. How quickly she had become both compass and anchor, helping him find his way and securing him in an alternate reality.

He'd proclaimed the country club date a bad idea. His social skills may have gone from nonexistent to passable but they were far from one hundred percent. Dorian had insisted he couldn't hide forever. What good was gaining knowledge if he never put his skills to the test? She said he had to venture out into the world someday, and dining at the club with her best friend was a nonthreatening place to start.

He'd better get used to being on his own. He was halfway through his training, and in another six weeks the terms of the contract Dorian had signed would be fulfilled. That's another reason he had to move out of her apartment. He'd become dependent on her. In six weeks he'd allowed her to become too important to him. Occupy too much of his heart.

He was a quick study, but she'd gotten under his skin, and another month and a half would not be nearly enough time to learn to live without her.

He watched the two women approach. Dorian had lost the visor and exchanged her chic golf outfit for a dress that flattered her slender figure. Her streaky blond hair swung loose, framing her face like a small golden cloud. Despite temperatures in the nineties, she looked as cool as a cantaloupe in her melon-colored dress. Her friend put a little too much wiggle in her walk, but Dorian, looking aloof and preoccupied, seemed to glide across the thick carpet.

Her distracted frown didn't mar the perfection of her face. Looking at her filled him with a rush of appreciation. She'd gone easy on the makeup and was just about the prettiest thing he'd ever seen. But something was wrong. Her full lips were firmly set and her delicately arched brows drawn together, as if someone had just handed her bad news.

He jumped to his feet and pulled out the ladies' chairs. Dorian had put him through his etiquette paces so many times, his actions were almost second nature by now. Remembering how to behave properly was like learning to drive. When he first started, he'd had to think about every step. Where to put his hands on the steering wheel. How to shift from first to second without grinding gears. How to let out the clutch without stalling the motor. And he could forget trying to talk while maneuvering through traffic. Getting from point A to point B had required his full attention, each action laboriously routed through intelligence central.

But with a little practice, driving had changed from a conscious activity to an almost unconscious one. The day came when he could get in a car and go where he wanted while thinking about other things along the way. Hopefully, appearing poised and confident would one day be second nature to him.

The waiter brought drinks for Dorian and Tiggy without them having to order. They seemed to take the special attention and service for granted. Briny asked for mineral water with a twist of lemon. He'd never quite gotten into the cocktail habit, having had to hide in the closet too many times when his father stumbled home drunk.

"Dorian, is everything all right?" he asked.

"Of course," she answered too quickly. "Why wouldn't everything be all right? Everything is fine. In fact, everything is peachy keen."

Her restless movements and curt comments made a lie of the chirpy disclaimer. Miss Coolly Collected was as edgy as a long-tailed cat in a room full of clog dancers. "I don't know, you seem kind of antsy."

Her look told him exactly what she thought of his choice of adjectives. "Don't worry, I'm fine. Probably just got too much sun." Refusing to look him in the eye, she studied the menu like a newly surfaced Dead Sea Scroll. How could he not worry? Something was clearly bothering her, and he wanted to get to the bottom of things. But when the waiter took their food order and left, Tiggy Moffat launched into gush-and-fawn mode.

"So, tell me, Brindon," she purred from across the table. "Have you had a chance to get a taste of Dallas night life yet?" She folded her arms on the table and leaned against them, thus cleverly creating cleavage where none had existed a moment before.

"We haven't gotten out much. We've been too busy with other things." He turned to Dorian for confirmation of their hectic schedule, but she didn't seem interested in taking part in the conversation. He couldn't tell if she was worried about something, annoyed at him or both.

"That's no fun." Tiggy toyed with a long strand of her dark hair.

According to one of the books Dorian had him read, that's what a woman did when she wanted a man to know she was attracted to him and available. He didn't need a book to recognize an undisguised come-on.

"You know what they say about all work and no play," she teased. "You don't want to get a reputation as a dull boy, do you?"

"Too late." He grinned. "I already am. Dull as ditch water. That's me."

"Modesty becomes you, but I'm sure you're not dull at all. In fact, I'll bet you can be downright exciting when you want to be."

Briny shrugged. "Not really. I'm more of a homebody. Just ask Dorian."

She looked up at the sound of her name. "He's not so much a homebody as he is a wanna-be hermit." She fussed with the flowers on the table and refused to look him in the eye. "I had to twist his arm to get him here today."

"You should definitely get out more," Tiggy purred. "Dallas has just about everything a man could want."

"Really?"

"There are some fabulous dance clubs here. Maybe we could check them out some time."

Dorian snorted. "Brindon doesn't dance."

Briny knew the women were friends, but surely Dorian would agree the brunette possessed the hint-taking capabilities of an aluminum siding salesman. Did she think he might take Tiggy up on her offer and was irritated because he wasn't good enough for her? After all, she had yet to introduce him to the rest of her crowd.

"And you call yourself a tutor?" Tiggy shot Dorian a quick look before leaning closer to Briny. "I'd be happy to give you some private lessons. Just say the word."

No probably wasn't in the woman's vocabulary. "Thanks for the offer, ma'am, but I'm sure Dorian will take care of me when the time comes. She's done a fine job of arranging classes and lessons so far."

"You can't learn to dance in a crowded class." When Tiggy sank her little white teeth into a topic, she hated to let go. "As with other physical activities, to get full benefit of the experience you need intensive one-on-one."

Back in Slapdown, in his other life, Briny had never imagined the day would come when he'd have to fend off the advances of a beautiful, sexy, rich woman. But that's what he was trying to do. Again he tried to make light of her suggestions. "I'm sure Dorian has something planned for me."

"Uh-huh." Tiggy's throaty tone packed a world of possibilities into two short syllables. "Knowing her, I'll just bet she does."

Dorian's eyes narrowed at the comment, but she didn't bother to reply. However when their salads arrived she did fatally stab a harmless cherry tomato with her fork. Now Briny knew she was upset. How many times had she instructed him never to stab tomatoes, but to slice them in two with his knife before eating them? She would have to be really riled to forget the basics.

"How did the golf game go today?" He directed his question to Dorian, but Tiggy answered.

"Dorian beat me by several strokes, as usual." The brunette sighed and gave her friend a wry look. "Our girl is very competitive, you know. If she decides she wants something, she goes after it. And she doesn't take prisoners."

Dorian scowled. "Tell us about your lesson, Brindon."

He admitted once he figured out what he was supposed to do with his irons, he had enjoyed whacking buckets of balls on the driving range. He wasn't sure the game qualified as a metaphor for life as Dorian had said, but it wasn't as bad as he'd expected. "The golf pro said I was a natural."

"He's right. You *are* a natural." Tiggy leaned in and gave him a look he could interpret only one way. *Come hither.* He tried to give her one she could understand without getting her feelings hurt. *No, thanks.*

"So are you two planning to attend the opening at Sabra's next week?" Tiggy asked.

"What?" Dorian's confusion proved she hadn't been paying attention.

"Liam's show at the gallery?" the brunette prompted. "You and Brindon are going, right? Everyone will be there."

"I don't know." Dorian gave up on her half-eaten salad. "Yes, maybe. Probably."

She remained sullen and twitchy. Briny was on his own, lobbing conversational balls back and forth across the table with Tiggy. Even when addressed directly, Dorian had a hard time focusing on the conversation and seemed relieved when the meal was finally over.

As they said goodbye and promised to meet at the gallery next week, Tiggy slipped Briny her phone number. Quickly, when no one was looking, he slid the piece of paper under his crumpled napkin.

Maybe on the way out he would give the unsuspecting waiter another tip.

Whatever you do, don't call that number.

Later in the evening Dorian discarded the cartons from their Chinese take-out meal. Since Brindon had moved in, she'd eaten more than she ever had in her life. The man was constantly hungry and couldn't go more than three or four hours between meals, even if he had snacks. She understood he hadn't gotten enough to eat as a child, but if she didn't control her own noshing, she would have to replace her size six clothes with a more comfortable size.

And if she didn't start reining in her out-of-control emotions, she was going to make a big mistake. She'd nearly lost control at the club today. Peeking into the living room, she saw Brindon stretched out on the sofa, his nose buried in a book. The old pair of Briny jeans he wore were faded and frayed at one knee. They hugged his slim hips and long legs like denim skin. His feet were bare, and a sleeveless, tank-type white undershirt stretched across his chest. His arms and shoulders were solid, strong and sinewy, but not bulky.

Reba sat on the floor beside him, her chin resting on his thigh. Without looking, Brindon reached out from time to time and scratched the dog's head. Dorian had finally gotten used to having the sweet old thing around and now understood Brindon's attachment to her. Reba was seventy pounds of canine devotion and love.

Love. There was that nasty word again. Since she had made the mistake of acknowledging the possibility this afternoon, the idea had nibbled through her brain like a caffeine-crazed rodent. She busied herself emptying the dishwasher and stacking clean dishes in the cupboards. Dammit. She'd spent half her life denying love even existed, so how had she let herself get caught in the web now?

Okay. For the sake of argument say love was a real, chemically induced emotion. Falling in love was hands-down the worst possible thing that could happen to her. And to Brindon. If she didn't believe in love, how could she *fall* into love? Falling implied a loss of control which ended with a heart-bruising landing. She didn't have to know calculus to put two and two together. The equation was simple enough for a C-minus art history major to understand.

Love equaled rejection plus pain, squared. A little lesson she had learned from her mother, a woman with an advanced degree in "Mismanagement of Affection."

She'd gotten all girly and jumpy today at the club, but maybe if she applied her unique perspective to the situation, she wouldn't be so frightened. The feeling that tripped her response switches when she so much as looked at Brindon was not love, she rationalized. The condition that made her think like the inside verse of a sappy Valentine card was not love, either. Nor was the jealousylike temptation to kick her best friend black and blue under the table at lunch today.

Not love at all.

Careful analysis would prove those disturbing symptoms were more likely due to a bad case of lust. A four-letter *L* word with its own unique set of complications, which was far more acceptable in the general scheme of things and a lot easier to deal with. According to Brindon's fairy-tale, one-woman-for-one-man philosophy, love was supposed to last forever. Sheesh, who could plan that far ahead?

Lust, on the other hand, was widely recognized as a temporary affliction with no long-term debilitating effects. Providing, of course, those involved were very, very careful.

She kicked the dishwasher door shut, then yelped and jumped around in an ouchy dance when pain zinged through her toe. She was definitely losing her grip. She had to stop thinking about such things. Lust might be easier than love but was just as dangerous. Disgusted with herself, Dorian knew succumbing to lust when she couldn't offer Brindon her heart made her just another predatory female out to satisfy number one.

Wasn't that why she'd been so irritated when her lifelong friend made a play for Brindon today? Tiggy didn't know anything about him. She certainly didn't love him. She was just attracted to his handsome face and sexy body.

His fifty million dollars didn't hurt, either. She wondered if Tiggy would still be attracted to him if she knew he was planning to give most of his lottery money away.

"Dorian?" Brindon called from the living room.

"Yes?" She grabbed a dish towel and wiped the spotless counter, in case he came to see what was keeping her so long.

"Aren't you about done in there?"

"Ah, in a minute."

"Hurry up. I have an idea."

Rats! He had a idea? She had hoped to escape to her room where she could deal with her own traitorous thoughts in private. His searching blue eyes had a way of blasting right through whatever facade she constructed. When he'd looked at her intently at lunch today, concern and worry etched on his handsome face, she had used every shred of self-control she had cultivated over the years not to stand up like a penitent and confess the truth of her feelings. Not only to Brindon, but to Tiggy, the waiter, a couple of busboys and a roomful of hungry diners.

Fortunately, running a slide show of French Impressionist paintings through her mind had proved a valuable deterrent to such self-destructive behavior.

When she finally went into the living room, she set a bowl of microwave popcorn on the table. "Thought you might like a snack."

He looked up from his book, a wide grin on his face. "Thanks." Swinging his long legs to the floor, he patted the couch cushion. "Want some?"

"What?" How did he know what she was thinking?

"Popcorn?" He reached for a handful and when she shook her head, he patted the cushion again. "Why don't you join me?"

She waffled. Couch bad. Chair across room better. Chair in the next room best of all. Sighing, she sank down beside him. "What is your idea?"

"We'll get to that in a minute. Let's talk first."

"About what?"

"The program. My progress. Where we want to go from here."

"Oh. I suppose you're right. All students expect to receive a report card periodically. For encouragement."

"I was always taught you have to reward effort," he teased. "That's how you keep the rat running through the maze."

She drew in a deep breath, and the enticing scent of his musky cologne came along for the ride. Men should not be allowed to smell that good.

"So how am I doing, teacher?" His lips tilted up crookedly, and the simple gesture drove her crazy. "And you're not allowed to say fine."

She had spent weeks looking at his lips, watching them flex through an extensive repertoire of grinning, pouting, curving, smiling, smirking and quirking. They had been nibbled in concentration, smacked with relish, licked unconsciously. She had seen all manner of food and drink pass between them. Seen them discover and relish new pleasures. In short, those were some hardworking lips. The only thing remaining to learn was how they felt pressed to hers. How they tasted. How accomplished they were at performing the job lips like his were meant to perform.

Was she asking too much?

"You've done well." She reached for a handful of popcorn to disguise the all-over flush heating her skin. "In fact, you have done so well, you probably don't need me anymore." There. Might as well lay her cards on the table.

He shook his head. "I don't think this Cinderella is ready for the ball yet. I've still got a long way to go. I need to start applying some of the things you've taught me."

"Okay, then." She slapped her hands on her thighs and jumped to her feet. All she could think about was what she *hadn't* taught him, subjects that definitely fell into the lust curriculum. "We'll begin with the art show next week, and you can dip your toe in the culture pool. Sounds like a plan. What do you say we call it a night?"

He laughed and took her hand, preventing her hasty retreat. "What's your hurry? It's only nine o'clock. You haven't even heard my idea yet."

"What idea? Have you come up with a way to solve the annoying problem of cell phone static?" She slipped her hand from his and folded her arms across her chest. She didn't like the way her skin tingled when he touched her. Yeah, right. She could be struck dead for such a lie. She liked the feeling too much.

"Not yet. I was hoping you could give me a dance lesson."

"Oh, no! I couldn't do that."

He did the cute-cocker-spaniel head tilt. "Why not? Don't you know how to dance?"

She could lie again. Say she had two left feet. But she'd taken years of dancing lessons. Ballet to modern jazz and everything in between. The dance floor was one of the few places she felt at home. She would have to do this. "I'm no slouch."

"Great! Your friend got me to thinking today."

"Really?" she asked dryly. "I've never known Tiggy to do *that* to a man before."

He ignored her cattiness and went on as though she hadn't interrupted. "Even if I don't like going to night clubs, there are sure to be occasions when I'll need to know my way around a dance floor. You *are* planning to take me to a few fancy affairs before you're done with me, aren't you?"

Dorian cleared the troublesome lump of desire from her throat. The man had said "take" him to affairs. Not have affairs with him. "Yes, of course."

"I'm glad we agree." He grabbed the arm of the sofa. "Help me rearrange the furniture, so we'll have room to bust some moves."

Bust some moves? When an adequate space had been

cleared, she opened the stereo cabinet. "Let me put the music on, and we'll take a test spin."

"Slow music."

His words put an abrupt halt to her search for music suitable for fast dancing. "Beg your pardon?"

"Put on a waltz or ballroom music. That's what I want to work on first. Then someday I want to try swing dancing. Like the jitterbug."

She blew out a frustrated breath. She'd planned to walk him through a few easy no-contact steps. Ballroom dancing required a bit more touching than she was willing to commit to at the moment. Her palm on his bare shoulder. His long-fingered hand on her back. Moving together until she felt the heat of his body. Until he felt the pounding of her nervous heart.

"Is anything wrong?" he asked.

"No. Nothing's wrong." She rifled through her music collection for appropriate tunes and loaded five disks onto the turntable. This blasted dancing lesson could go on a long time without interruption.

Things could be worse. He could have suggested learning the tango. Or the lambada. The direction her thoughts were taking, any dancing was sure to be dirty dancing.

Since love was not an option, maybe she should stop fighting the lust factor and give in to her bad-girl destiny. She had tried to be good the past few weeks, but she would never be as kind or generous or thoughtful as Brindon. She didn't have the genetic potential. She never would have thought to give a truck to a waitress at a bus stop. Not in a million years.

And truth be told, she *did* make donations to The Children's Development Fund so she could attend the gala. Who was she kidding? No graham-cracker-eating munchkin would ever willingly sit in her lap. On the other hand, Brindon was the kind of man who would want lots of tots, all bearing his remarkable DNA. Over the past few days she'd realized he would make a wonderful father, and his cute little babies deserved a wonderful mother, too.

She would never be that woman. The odds weren't in her

favor. She had every chance of being as big a failure at parenting as her own mother. She wanted Brindon's respect, but had trouble pretending to be something she wasn't. Campaigning for "Most Likely to be Canonized" was too stressful, and Dorian didn't do stress. She caused stress. The sooner she dropped the charade, the sooner Brindon would realize how unlovable she was.

Then, when the terms of their contract had been met, there would be nothing binding them together. He could continue his foolish search for one perfect woman to love forever. Letting him go would hurt. But not letting go would hurt him more.

In a moment, smooth orchestral music poured from the speakers. Briny stood in the middle of the cleared space and waited for Dorian to come to him. He'd never seen her so reticent. As though she couldn't stand the thought of him taking her into his arms. Which wasn't so hard to understand. No matter how much spit and shine she'd put on him, he was still just an unschooled, unsophisticated oil rig foreman from Slapdown.

What was that proverb he'd read? Familiarity breeds contempt. The better a person knew someone, the less he respected them. But maybe it meant a person couldn't be fooled into thinking someone was something they were not. Back home people said just because a kitten is born in the stove, doesn't mean it's a biscuit.

In the beginning he'd believed if he learned enough, looked the part and talked properly, he could bridge the gap between his world and Dorian's. A fine bit of what the psychology book called self-delusion. The gap between their worlds was the Grand Canyon, and there weren't enough books or designer clothes in Texas to fill it up.

Still, he'd been hopeful. Until today at lunch, when Tiggy Moffat made her play for him. Though she hadn't said anything, Dorian had become increasingly agitated as the meal progressed. She knew him better than anyone, so obviously, if she didn't think he was good enough for her best friend, she certainly wouldn't welcome his advances. She'd worked hard to be nice, but her actions were clear. She didn't want him going out with her friend.

If familiarity did indeed breed contempt, why couldn't it breed desire? He'd never read that in any of his assigned books, but just because it hadn't happened before didn't mean it was impossible. He believed in luck. He'd won the lottery, hadn't he? He was living proof. Miracles did happen. Fairy tales could come true.

If he spent the next few weeks being the best darned millionaire former oil rig foreman she'd ever become familiar with, Dorian might realize he could be more than a pupil. Maybe his feelings of attachment would evolve into something more permanent. And what better time to start than tonight, while he had a legitimate excuse to hold her close.

Chapter Eight

Dorian wasted as much time as she could adjusting the sound system's bass, volume and balance controls. When she turned around, Brindon was standing patiently in the middle of the space they had cleared. Wearing worn jeans and an old-fashioned tank-type undershirt, with his hair mussed and his feet bare, he looked more endearing than any man had a right to look.

His shoulders and eyebrows rose at the same time. "So what do you want me to do?"

A simple question, but more than one lascivious answer popped into her hormone-saturated mind. How could she answer honestly when what she really wanted was out of the question? "Uh, first we assume the position."

Why did everything she think or say have a double meaning?

"Yes, Drill Sergeant!" His joke was obviously meant to put her at ease, but couldn't keep a little shiver from dancing up her spine as she stepped into his arms. Was she nervous because she knew where an innocent activity like this could lead? Or because she knew she couldn't let it lead anywhere? She took a steadying breath and managed to get their bodies aligned without much trouble. She explained in a neutral *tutor* voice that for instruction purposes, she would lead for now.

"That's fine with me." He took her proffered hand and grinned. "You know what you're doing."

No, she didn't. If she did, she would have found him the best dance instructor in Dallas and sent him off for private lessons. If she had, the thought of standing in the circle of his arms wouldn't be making her weak in the knees. Why did he have to be so trusting? Didn't he realize he was delivering himself into the clutches of a wicked heiress with hanky-panky on the brain? When he pressed his palm to her back, his touch ignited a slow flame that licked its way through her body.

She fought to control the fire as she demonstrated a basic ballroom two-step. Her pulse pounded from too much Brindon, much too close. She felt the gentle rise and fall of his chest as he breathed. Maybe if he put a shirt on over his tee…so her palm wasn't resting on the warm skin of his shoulder…she could concentrate on the dance instead of the man.

She pulled back by forcing her thoughts onto the task at hand, walking him through the steps again. She wasn't surprised he picked up on them quickly, he'd proven to be a fast learner in every subject he'd studied. Incredibly light on his feet for a big man, he possessed an athlete's natural grace that instilled his movements with unexpected sensuality. Even his bare feet were sexy, long and narrow, with a high instep and perfectly formed toes.

Lordy, if his toes turned her on, she was in deep trouble.

Dorian looked up from his disturbing feet and caught him watching her intensely, his blue eyes as warm and welcoming as a summer sky.

"You have excellent body control." Teacher commending student. Nothing else. "Were you ever into sports?"

"I played a lot of hooky."

The music swelled dramatically, and she led him through a twirl around the floor. "Field or ice?"

He smiled. "Not hockey. Hooky. You know, skipping school?"

"Oh. Right." Yes, she knew about that. She'd nearly been

expelled from Creighton during her senior year for sneaking off to New York City for the weekend. What lesson had she learned during an extended period of house arrest? Play with fire; get burned.

Brindon was easily the tallest man she had ever danced with, and she was dismayed that their bodies fit together like two pieces of a jigsaw puzzle. It probably wasn't a politically correct feminist ideal, but Dorian had always envied small women who could nestle their heads on their dance partners' chests, protected by superior size and strength. At five feet ten inches, she had seldom experienced that feeling. Until now. Until Brindon. She felt safe in the circle of his arms. But she couldn't make him her haven from life's storms. That would be asking too much.

Old memories surfaced as she led him through the familiar dance steps, bringing with them the acrid taste of rejection. She recalled a much-admired gym teacher at Creighton who had cut her down in front of the class by remarking that if Dorian wasn't careful she would bulk up to Amazon proportions. A gawky thirteen-year-old, she'd taken those harsh words to heart. She couldn't control her genetically determined growth pattern, so she had concentrated on watching her weight. Before long, dieting and denial had become a way of life. Only by luck and willpower had she avoided the chronic eating disorders to which many of her classmates succumbed.

Later, when she realized designer clothes looked better on the tall, stick-figure models than on the average-size women who purchased them, she had worked at staying thin and wearing beautiful, expensive clothing like others worked at careers. Many believed pure vanity motivated her, but they were wrong. Fear was at the heart of everything she did. If she lost control or gave in to her appetites, the gym teacher's prophecy would come true. Her adult life would be as unhappy as her adolescence.

She'd since done much to reinvent herself, but she had never forgotten the gangling child or the ugly-duckling teen she'd been. Though many years had passed, the memories were always close, easily resurrected by the haunting strains of familiar music.

Nightmarish cotillions and proms. Most of the boys from Haverton, a neighboring prep school, had not completed their adolescent growth spurts by ninth grade. During the obligatory dances their pimple-dotted faces had leered into her newly developed bosom, and she had longed to run from the room like Cinderella at 11:59 p.m.

Forced to endure the humiliation, she'd soon discovered squeaky-voiced taunts of "stringbean" and "treetop" couldn't hurt her if she didn't care about the boys who made them. Teachers who criticized her for not applying herself to studies couldn't wound her if she spurned academic success. Cassandra's lack of interest and habitual absence from school activities couldn't devastate her if she didn't need her mother's love. Not even the forced separation from her grandmother could make her cry if she didn't care.

Life cannot hurt you if you don't need anything. Wanting things was fine. Needing people was not. Had she really adopted such a sad, defeatist philosophy?

"So, how am I doing?" Brindon's teasing words rounded up Dorian's wandering thoughts and sent them scurrying back into the dark where they belonged.

"Very well." They had worked through the box step and a simple fox-trot. The ease with which he slid barefoot around the floor made her job a pleasure. "You're good. Are you sure you haven't done this before?"

"Just country dancing in beer joints and honky-tonks. Nothing like this one two three, slide, one two three. If you want, I'll teach you how to line dance sometime."

The offer pleased her more than she cared to admit. It meant their time together might last a little longer. "I'd like that."

"We'd have to get some different music." His rakish grin elicited a ripple of pleasure that teased her senses. "You can't do the Electric Slide to Strauss."

She laughed to cover her unease. "No, I wouldn't think so. Good catch on the music. Do you recognize the piece?"

"Yes, teacher, I do. I believe we are currently dancing to 'The Blue Danube' waltz."

With his sharp mind and quick wit, in other circumstances, Brindon might have become a scholar. Dorian was chilled to think of what he could have accomplished with the educational opportunities she'd frittered away. Given half a chance and an ounce of encouragement, he would have certainly achieved success. But instead of using his knowledge to build empires and stockpile money for himself, he would have worked to better the world. Because he possessed the same compassion and unselfish altruism as the girl in school who had dreamed of being a doctor.

Dorian admired him for not allowing himself to become a victim of his unfortunate childhood. Unlike her, Brindon did not allow the past to color his future. His fortunes had changed, and he was enthusiastically making up for lost time.

He had hired her to teach him. But she was the one who'd learned the most. Like a piece of film coming gradually into focus, understanding dawned and Dorian finally appreciated his desire to share with others all that he'd received. Dammit. She'd hoped to chalk her feelings up to lust and to deny anything less selfish. But knowing Brindon only made her love him more because he had taught her how. As much as she tried to deny the truth, love was not easily thwarted and did not take to being ignored.

All she had to do was devise a self-improvement plan for herself. One that, once completed, would make her the person she wanted to be. Maybe then she would be entitled to happiness. And Brindon would learn to love her.

He spun her out with a dramatic flourish and was mortified when he stepped on her toe. "Gosh darn it, I'm sorry. I guess it's a good thing I didn't put my shoes on. I could have broken something. Did I hurt you?"

"No. You didn't hurt me." She had hurt herself by wanting a man she did not deserve and by being too blind to know what to do. Now she knew. She could change.

"Because I'd hate to hurt you, Dori."

Dori. She liked him to call her that. The nickname inspired

and gave her hope. Dori sounded like a good woman. A sweet, unselfish woman, content to love her prince and bear his children and grow old with him, sharing the sunset from an ivory tower somewhere in a fairy-tale land. Dori would not be afraid of her feelings; she would embrace them.

Dorian wasn't Dori. Yet. Maybe if things had been different, if she had made other choices, taken a higher path, she might have grown up to be Dori. Longing would not make it so, and that was what she'd been doing. To turn the tide, she would have to expend more effort than she had ever been willing to expend before. But she could do it. The prospect of making herself over into a woman Brindon might love thrilled and terrified her.

The musical selection ended and another began, one with a faster tempo requiring fancier footwork. Brindon startled her by assuming command. "I think I've got the hang of things now, teacher. Time for me to lead." With the simple steps he'd just mastered, he led her in a double-time sweep around the floor, the added momentum forcing him to hold her more closely. The heat from his body relaxed her tense muscles like a deep massage.

Brindon leaned down and spoke into her ear, his breathy whisper releasing a purl of desire. "Do you have any slow music in your collection? Maybe something composed in this century?"

"Why do you ask?"

"I want to do something besides waltz."

She swallowed hard. She wanted to do something else, too, but she wasn't thinking of slow dancing. What she wanted to do involved no vertical movement at all. "I'll see what I can find." She willed the lusty thoughts from her mind before they could sabotage her new resolve. She scanned the CD tower, and when she found what she was looking for, opened the carousel, removed Strauss and dropped a disc containing Tony Bennett's greatest hits onto the turntable. His signature tune floated out of the speakers as he crooned about leaving his heart in San Francisco.

Brindon lowered the lights and touched a match to the collection of plumeria-scented candles on the mantel.

"What are you doing?" Dorian hadn't meant her words to sound accusing, but she was determined to behave nobly and refused to be sidetracked by cheap tricks. Like Sleeping Beauty recently awakened from a hundred-year sleep, Dorian had a long to-do list before she allowed the prince to charm her.

She watched Brindon light the other candles scattered around the room. She might be mixing fairy-tale metaphors, but a frog's transformation into a prince had finally shaken her out of suspended animation. He'd given her a glimpse of what her life might yet be, not by kissing her but by setting a good example.

"What do you think I'm doing?"

"You can't learn anything in the dark." She had to keep him focused on dancing. She couldn't lose control now, not when she was filled with new hope.

"Oh, you'd be surprised what a person can learn with the lights turned low." He caught her hand and yanked her close in an overwrought parody of a late-show Fred Astaire and Ginger Rogers routine. Laughing, he dipped her low and bent over her until his mouth was only inches from her own. "How did you like that move, teacher?"

"You seem to have the basic steps down." She forced the words past lips tingling with anticipation. "Maybe we should call it a night. I don't think you need me to show you anything else."

"Yes, I do." He reeled her out of the dip and snuggled her body close to his, their curves and hollows fitting together in imitation of intimacy. His blue eyes went smoky in the candlelight, and his voice dropped to a timbre that filled her with desire. He had a voice women dreamed of hearing in the dark. "A man can't dance without a partner."

Good thing he wasn't a mind reader, because she was shamed by the thought of how much nicer the closeness would be without all the clothes between his warm skin and hers. She shook those thoughts from her mind. This was not the time. She couldn't settle for lust when love might be within her grasp.

He held her close, one hand firmly pressing her back while the other folded around hers to rest on his chest. Beneath her palm, she felt the rhythm of his heart racing ahead of the music. He bent his head, and his lips brushed her neck. "We make a good team, Dori."

"Don't call me that." Her whispered plea caught in her throat like a sob. Not yet. Not until she had earned it.

He stroked her back, and she shivered with pleasure. "You're trembling like a wet wren," he said. "What's wrong?"

"Nothing." Everything. She had never succeeded at anything in her life. Why did she think she could remake herself in the image of the woman she wanted to be?

"Can't you tell me what's troubling you?" His quiet question made her think he might be a mind reader, after all.

"No." She couldn't tell him she wanted to love him, but was afraid she'd hurt him. She couldn't tell him she longed to be the kind of woman he needed, but worried she was destined to be like her mother. Only interested in herself. And she especially couldn't tell him she wanted to dive headfirst into the pool of strange and wonderful feelings he aroused, but was floundering in deep, uncharted waters.

Doubt frayed her resolve. What made her think Brindon could love her? She was an emotional cripple.

She'd have to send her mother a thank-you card for that.

A lone tear slid down her cheek before she could blink it away. Brindon danced her closer to the candlelight, if their intimate full-body press qualified as dancing, and turned the full force of his electric blue gaze on her.

His eyes narrowed in concern. "Did I say something wrong?"

The hesitancy in his words shot straight to her heart, and she rushed to answer. "No."

"I'm a good listener. Want to talk about what's bothering you?"

"No."

"What can I do to help?"

"Nothing." Another tear quickly followed the trail blazed by the first. Dammit! What was wrong with her?

Brindon tipped up her face and gently touched his lips to the trembling tear, taking the salty drop into himself the way he seemed to want to take away her sadness. Tony Bennett sang about growing accustomed to her face, and they swayed to the gentle rhythm, their bodies sliding together in an intoxicating caress.

Brindon kissed her cheek where the tear had been, then his mouth slipped down to her chin and up to the tiny indention above her lip. She sighed with pleasure and regret. She shouldn't be doing this now, but she was powerless to stop. She was weak. She'd waited all her life for joy and anticipation to turn her insides as soft and gooey as the center of a fancy chocolate. And here it was. Special delivery. When she closed her eyes, Brindon kissed her eyelids, first one, then the other, feathery touches so light she sensed rather than felt them.

The music played on, but they stopped pretending to dance. They stood locked together, lost in discovery, unable to move, unwilling to try. Before he could kiss every square inch of her face and drive her crazy in the process, Dorian slipped her arms around Brindon's neck and pulled his lips onto hers. She moaned with pleasure as he led an assault on her senses.

There was no hesitancy in the mouth that slanted over hers. His lips were both firm and soft. Both giving and taking. Just as she'd expected, his hardworking lips knew exactly what to do. When to apply pressure, when to let up. When to nibble, when to tug. When to insist, when to coax. But as talented as his lips were, they could take lessons from his tongue. That amazing part of him dipped into her mouth, gently teasing at first, then so slow and drugging she couldn't have remained on her feet if he hadn't held her up.

He had a dozen little tricks through which he lazily worked his magic on her. His hands soon got into the act. They stroked, rubbed, caressed. Her arms, her back, her neck. The volatile mix of desire and longing he created would surely make her spontaneously combust.

Several minutes passed in sweet abandon. Brindon's athletic lips showed no sign of tiring, and he seemed in full agreement with Tony's warbled recommendation that anything goes. Dorian didn't know which startled her more. Brindon's hunger. Or her own.

Without releasing his hold on her, he worked his way to the couch. He lowered them onto it and settled against the cushions. Cradling her on his lap, he tangled his hand in the hair at the nape of her neck. As much as she hated to lose contact, she broke the lip lock before she could be swept away and buried her face against his chest. The sharp scent of detergent and bleach lingering in his snow-white T-shirt was more intoxicating than designer cologne.

He rubbed her arm. "We got carried away there for a moment."

"Yes, we did."

"I'm kinda wondering where we're going from here." His words were tense, as though forced past his lips. "I don't know if the destination I have in mind is the one you want."

"I'm sorry," she whispered. "I shouldn't have started something we can't finish."

He sighed. "I don't think it's real clear who started what. But I know something is bothering you. We can talk if you want."

"I can't." How could she explain the clash between her needs and wants to the object of her confusion? She didn't fully understand herself, but she knew making love with him now would spoil everything. If she succumbed to selfishness before proving herself to him, she'd blow her chance for that happily-ever-after he believed in.

How could she have thought lust was easier than love?

"Cry it out, Dori."

"Don't be silly. I don't cry."

"What's this?" He touched his fingertip to another traitorous tear.

"Optical fluid, necessary to keep the eye from drying out and turning into a raisin."

"We all cry. There's no shame in tears." He was not put off by her distancing tactics.

"I gave them up a long time ago."

"Tell me why." He smoothed an errant strand of hair from her face, his fingers brushing the skin of her jaw lightly. "Tell me what scares you. If you shine a light on the monsters, sometimes they go away."

How could she reveal the shameful secret she'd kept for thirteen years? Half her life. Rattling its cage wouldn't make her feel better. Or would it?

Brindon rocked her against his wide, warm chest as if she were a child. He wrapped his arms around her and stroked her hair. "Everything will be all right," he whispered.

"You don't know."

"Nothing you can say will make me think less of you."

"I've never told anyone."

"I'm here for you, Dori. You can tell me anything. I won't turn away or judge you, honey."

No one had ever made promises like that before. Her heart ached with love for him. Love that would only hurt him and hurt her and drive them apart. When Tony Bennett started singing about a poor little rich girl, a soul-deep sigh escaped Dorian's lips, battering down the dam that had held back her pent-up emotions for so long.

"I stopped believing in love a long time ago." She hadn't thought she could reveal the secret she had kept so long, locked in her soul. But Brindon's promises were the key that opened the door, releasing her words in a wild stampede. "Love tore my family apart. My father wasted his love on a woman who wouldn't—or couldn't—love him. Love cost him his life."

"Tell me." Brindon held her close, sheltering her in his arms.

"The doctors ruled his overdose an accident, but he was too smart to bungle anything as simple as medication." Bitterness, still strong after so many years, tainted her words.

"He was bedridden. ALS had destroyed the motor pathways to his muscles, but his mind was as sharp as ever. He planned his death and ended his life with blood-chilling resolve." She shuddered and a sob tore down her control.

"My God, Dori." Brindon's arms tightened around her as if he could prevent the truth from tearing her apart. She was afraid to reveal the secret she'd hidden from everyone but herself, but his gentle touch gave her courage to reach back into the murky past.

She had watched her mother work up convincing tears at her father's graveside. "Cassandra's black-garbed, grieving-widow routine might have fooled others, even Granny Pru. But I didn't buy her act for a second. I knew the truth. My father was dead because he'd loved her, and she didn't deserve his love."

Dorian stilled and focused her gaze on a flickering candle across the room as she recalled that horrible time. "I heard my parents arguing, two days before the 'accidental' overdose. Cassandra, always the drama queen, screamed she couldn't take it anymore."

She laughed, but there was no mirth in the sound. "She couldn't take it? A devastating illness had turned my father's life into a living hell but had scarcely put a crimp in hers. Dad lay in his lonely bed in a darkened room while her sparkly life whirled on without him. He went to doctors. She went to parties. He made the rounds of specialists. She made the rounds of social events."

"Go on." Brindon's voice was steady, calm. Reassuring.

"It's important to keep up appearances, you know." Dorian's words were scornful. "She entertained her friends with little thought for my dad who had been struck down in the prime of life."

"What happened?" Brindon urged. "You haven't told anyone, but you can tell me."

So she did. She had to. She'd been thirteen, home from Creighton for the holidays. She'd gone shopping with Tiggy and was supposed to spend the night. But her friend had become ill, and the Moffats' driver had dropped Dorian off at home.

"I let myself in and started up the stairs. Then I heard my mother's raised voice coming out of daddy's sick room on the first floor. His voice, weakened by disease, was so breathy and quiet I had to lean against the closed door of what had once been my father's study. I eavesdropped because that was the only way I felt connected to my family." Over the years she'd become a master at listening secretly to conversations that did not include her. She recalled that last conversation word for word.

"I...just need you...to stay with me for a...few hours," her father said. "Please."

"I told you, I've made plans. You shouldn't have given the nurse the afternoon off."

"Can't you change them...for me...just this once?"

"This once? Don't you understand my whole life has changed?"

"I'm...sorry."

"So am I, John. I'm sorry you're ill. I'm sorry you will never get better. I'm sorry your life is over. But mine is not. I'm healthy. I have needs. Why should I give up everything?"

"I don't ask...you to give up anything...for me." Dorian knew how much the words cost her father. In recent days, breathing had become difficult for him, and the doctors said he would soon need to be placed on a ventilator. She'd asked her grandmother what that meant, and Granny Pru had explained a ventilator was a machine that breathed for people whose lungs no longer worked properly.

"No. You don't ask. You just lie there, paralyzed and—"

"Useless?" The whispered word sliced through the closed door like a hatchet.

"You said it, not me."

"I love...you, Cassandra. I have...always...loved you."

"You haven't 'loved' me for nearly a year. But don't worry. I've found someone to take care of my needs. But as long as you're still...sick, I can't move on or have a real life. I can't stand living in limbo like this!"

Her father didn't say anything for a long time. Dorian slumped against the door, her stomach churning with sick fury. She wanted to rush into the room. Strike her mother's beautiful, haughty face until she took back her hurtful words. But she couldn't move. She was a wounded child, shocked by the betrayal of a mother who withheld her love. And faced with the loss of a father who loved too much.

"Do you want…a divorce?" he had asked at last.

Cassandra had laughed then, and Dorian could still hear the cold, heartless sound. "A divorce? Be serious, John. That would hardly be financially prudent, would it? I may not be faithful, but I am patient. I can wait."

"For me to…die?"

"We both know it's only a matter of time."

"Maybe you won't have to…wait for long." He'd spoken the words so quietly Dorian had strained to hear them.

That's when she'd fled the house, convinced her father's illness had progressed and the end was near. Until that moment she had childishly prayed for his recovery, believed the doctors would find a miracle cure and restore him to her. She had escaped to a nearby park where she had curled up under a picnic table in the cold, gray light of the worst day of her life.

She'd wept until her tears had washed away all hope. When there were no tears left to shed, she had forced herself to return to the empty house that would never be her home. Slipping into her father's room, she'd found him asleep and had sat beside his bed all night, her head resting on his blanket. If he woke up, she would tell him how much she loved him. Maybe she could make up for the things her mother had said.

"Forty-eight hours later, three days before Christmas, my father died." Dorian spoke quietly as Tony asked the musical question: "Are You Havin' Any Fun?"

Not really.

"I'm sorry, Dori. No little girl should have to go through what your mother put you through." She saw her pain reflected on the smooth planes of Brindon's face.

"They said the overdose was a mix-up with his medication,

but it had taken him that long to accumulate enough pills to end his life. No one else would admit the truth.''

''You knew.''

''Yes. I knew the truth. And I kept the secret to protect my mother.'' The burden had weighed heavily on her child's heart. She'd felt disloyal to her father and unsure her mother deserved her loyalty. Especially when Cassandra turned away after John's death, unable or unwilling to offer comfort to her only child.

Standing between her and her grandmother at her father's grave, Dorian had made a dry-eyed vow. At thirteen she had declared herself done with crying. And loving. Love hurt. But not being loved couldn't hurt her if she didn't care. She had vowed never to love anyone. Ever.

Her amazing feelings for Brindon had given her hope that she might yet heal her wounded emotions and lay the past to rest for good. Could she truly have a future with a man like Brindon? Or had she deluded herself into thinking love could be more powerful than pain?

Chapter Nine

Candlelight flickered, Briny held Dorian, and Tony Bennett warbled his last song. When the final note faded, the sound of their quiet breathing filled the room. Her story had broken his heart, but it had not shattered her control. She'd rejected his advice to "cry it out," and he hurt to think she still didn't feel safe enough with him to let down the barriers she'd built around her emotions.

"You and your mother never talked about what happened?" Asking was a formality. If Dorian understood her father's suicide, her mother understood it, as well. Shameful secrets had sprung up between them, fed on their silence and destroyed the love they might have shared.

"I don't have 'talks' with my mother." Dorian's voice was cold. "She hasn't been interested in anything I've had to say since I learned to talk."

"What about your grandmother? Did you speak to her?"

"And tell her what? That she lost her son because her unfaithful daughter-in-law told him she was tired of waiting for him to die?"

"No." He stroked her hair. "You couldn't tell her that."

"Granny Pru has about given up on me. I'm a big disappointment to her."

"I doubt that," he protested.

"True enough. She loves me, but she wants me to be more like my father, the beloved son she lost. Unfortunately, I'm too much like the daughter-in-law she despises."

"You're nothing like your mother." He spoke with conviction. Instinct told him she had little in common with Cassandra Burrell.

"How do you know?" She looked at him, and he wished he could rid her eyes of the despair he saw there. "I look like her. I act like her. I've never done a useful thing in my adult life. I'm spoiled, selfish, manipulating. I think I *am* very much like her."

"Just because you share her eye color doesn't mean you're fated to repeat her mistakes." He brushed her cheek. "You can be whatever you want."

"And I suppose all the experts are wrong. Nature and nurture have nothing to do with the formation of character."

"We can overcome both nature and nurture."

"What about fate? Destiny?"

"What about free will?"

"Can I ask you something?" She moved out of his arms as if putting a little distance between them would aid her argument. She sat at the end of the sofa in white linen-cotton pants and a silky black top, her long legs tucked under her.

Briny missed the soft weight of her body and fought the urge to pull her back into his arms. If anyone needed comfort, Dorian did. He could offer it, but he couldn't make her accept it. "Sure. Anything."

"Will you tell me the truth?"

"I always tell the truth."

"Why did you kiss me back?"

She sure knew how to cut to the chase, which was one of the things he admired most about her. She didn't have a coy bone in her body. "I don't think I could have *not* kissed you," he admitted honestly. "I've been itching to taste those sweet, sassy lips since that first day in Malcolm's office."

"Really?" Her eyes narrowed. "That means you were attracted by my appearance."

"No, I wasn't." He'd been drawn by her confidence, and by her cocksure attitude that she was superior in every way to most people in the universe. He smiled. How could he explain that? Especially now that he knew how uncertain she really was.

"Well, you weren't attracted to my mind. Nor my personality, because I wasn't very nice to you that day."

He laughed. "You were…"

"Condescending? Snooty? Snotty? All of the above?"

He grinned. He had thought she was all those things. "I was going to say patronizing. I didn't understand what the word meant then, but I do now."

"You know a lot more now than you did few weeks ago."

One thing he knew for sure. He could love her, if she'd let him. He'd long suspected it, but when she'd responded to his kiss, the revelation had come as sudden and thorough as a good sandblasting. Her desire had matched his in the moments before she'd pulled away from it. "You're my tutor. You should take credit for the knowledge I've gained."

"No. You get all the credit." She clutched a tasseled pillow to her chest. "There's something you don't understand. When you hired me, I thought I was supposed to turn you into a spoiled, bored, selfish cynic."

"And?"

"I failed."

Briny stroked his upper lip. He'd almost forgotten the mustache that had grown there so long. He didn't miss it now, because it no longer seemed a part of who he was. "I've changed a lot."

"You haven't changed at all," she countered. "You've grown, learned new things, refined your tastes. But you're the same person. You're still kind. Generous. Idealistic." She frowned, as though something troubling had just occurred to her. "Hmm."

"What?"

"Maybe people *can't* really change. Maybe they can only

enhance what is already there." She made it sound like the saddest conclusion ever reached.

"Why do you think that?" he asked.

"My father's illness didn't change him. Neither did my mother's rejection. He loved her until the end. Cassandra had everything, a devoted husband and a child who needed her. Yet the things we could give, love and security, could not change or satisfy her."

"I told you not to compare yourself to her." Briny didn't like the direction the conversation was taking. Dorian was manipulating the facts to support her lack of faith in herself. And he was getting in over his head. How could he hold his own in a philosophical debate?

"I took a pottery class once," she said. "I thought I was an artist because I could turn a lump of ugly gray clay into something beautiful."

"That's what you did with me," he said to lighten the mood. "I was a pretty big lump when we met."

She shook her head and pounded the pillow with her fist. "You don't understand. I know now that I didn't turn the clay into anything. The vase was already inside. All I did was unlock the potential by spinning a wheel."

"And there's a difference?"

"A big difference. A sculptor's chisel doesn't change a slab of marble into a statue. He finds the statue in the stone by chipping away everything that is not a part of the statue."

"You have the art degree, not me. I don't understand."

"The most talented potter in the world cannot turn a sack of sand into a vase. The potential isn't there." She sighed, whether from resignation or frustration, Briny couldn't decide. "Not even Michaelangelo could find a David in a chunk of slate."

"But people aren't made of stone," he argued gently. "They're organic, always changing. One of the books I read said we even grow a whole new skin every seven years. What makes us different from every other creature on the planet is our logic, our reason and the ability to become whatever we want."

"And you believe that?" Unmistakable derision told him she did not.

"If I didn't believe, I wouldn't be here."

"Where did you come from, Brindon? I want to know."

"I was born and raised in west Texas. I told you that."

She smiled. "Where did your potential come from? How did you become the incredible man you are? Your mother died when you were small."

"Yet I lived. There had to be a reason for that. An elderly gentleman had a stroke at the wheel and his car plowed into us on the way to Sunday school. Mom was driving and died instantly. I was in the back seat and barely got a scratch. Of course, I didn't think about such things then, I was too young. But later I decided I must have survived for a reason, and my job was to figure out what that reason was."

"But your father abandoned you."

"Dad had some problems. I don't blame him for falling apart. He loved my mother with everything he had. Losing her ripped his heart out."

"He left you alone for days at a time, with nothing to eat."

"Other people took me in," he said. "Fed me. Clothed me. Sent me to school. The house parents at Los Huerfanos were wonderful. Mom Appleton used to tell me I was her favorite. Out of the six boys in the cottage, I was the one she expected to do great things. I'd get in trouble, and she'd quietly remind me to stay on the path. If I felt sorry for myself, she'd point out how lucky I was. She set the limits, and I tested them. I let her down plenty of times, but she never stopped believing in me. Never stopped telling me I was destined for bigger things."

"She sounds like a wonderful person."

"Smart, too. Later, I realized she probably told all the boys the same thing, those who came before me and those who came after. But I wanted to believe her."

"That's what made you different."

"Maybe. I had to leave the home when I turned eighteen. I bawled like a baby. Didn't want to go. I had no other place in the world."

"What did you do?"

"Pop Appleton talked the foreman at Chaco Oil into giving me a job. He stood right there and told the boss I might not look like much, but I had a good heart and a strong back. He said I was honest and would work hard."

"And?"

"I did. I couldn't very well make a liar out of Pop. Not after he went out on a limb for me like that."

Dorian's face dropped into her hands. After a moment she looked up, her eyes glistening with tears she probably wouldn't shed. "You make me ashamed of myself."

"I didn't mean to do that," he protested. "You asked and I—"

"Don't worry. You've confirmed what I already knew. You have always been a big wonderful lump of potential, Brindon. Unlike me, who is just an expensive sack of designer sand."

"That's not true." He folded his arms and tucked his hands against his body. He wanted to reach out to her, but he had to let her make the next move. How he handled the next few minutes might determine their whole future. If they had one. "You've never tried to accomplish anything, because no one ever expected you to. No one has believed in you. And the worst of it is, you've never believed in yourself."

Her laughter contained little mirth. "For a moment, I actually believed I could change. You made me think I could. But I was just kidding myself."

"I believe in you, Dori."

"Don't say that." She tossed the pillow at him, and he caught it on the fly. "Not if you don't mean it."

"I always mean what I say. I—"

"Don't make promises. I'd hate to have to hold you to them."

"And I don't make promises I can't keep."

"Maybe you should move on," she told him. "Get your own place. Start living the life you've learned about. You don't need me anymore."

"Whoa, now. Slow down." He held up one hand. "You signed a contract agreeing to tutor me for three months. You have six weeks to go before you're out from under that obligation.''

She looked at him, her eyes dark with doubt. "You wouldn't hold me to our contract, would you?"

To keep from losing her? Damned straight he would. He needed time to help her discover the potential locked inside her, time for her to learn love is the greatest gift anyone can give. "You wouldn't seriously try to weasel out of our contract, would you?"

She hesitated, as if assessing his sincerity. "I'm willing to bow out gracefully."

"I'm not willing to let you." He needed time to convince her that change was not only possible but inevitable.

"We can't go on living together like this," she said. "Not after tonight. People don't change, but situations do. We crossed a line. Things are…"

"Different?" Briny knew fires had started smoldering tonight, fires that needed careful tending to keep from burning out of control and destroying the trust he'd worked so hard to build between them. "But a deal's a deal."

Four weeks ago he had believed Dorian beyond his reach. In that time he'd progressed from worshipping her from afar to holding her close. From thinking he didn't have a chance with her to knowing he did. He'd already climbed halfway up the glass hill. They could have the fairy tale if she didn't run away from her feelings.

"What are we going to do?" she asked tentatively.

"I've taken advantage of your hospitality long enough." He had to step back, because pressing her too soon would be a mistake. But he wouldn't give up. "I'll find a place. Reba and I will move out. But I insist you honor our contract. I still have a lot to learn."

She seemed to mull over the idea. "I did sign an agreement. I probably should have read the fine print."

"I have a copy somewhere. I'll find it if you want."

"No need. I trust you."

"Good."

"When faced with problems in the past, I've always taken

the easy way out.'' She pulled her knees up and hugged them. ''I don't think the question ever arose as to whether I was doing the right or honorable thing before.''

''No time like the present,'' he prompted with a grin.

''I'd like to start now, if I haven't waited too long.''

''It's never too late.'' If he could continue spending time with Dorian, Briny hoped he might yet help her find the self-esteem her mother had carelessly destroyed. He couldn't give her the gift of pride, nor could he force it on her. But maybe he could show her the way, as others had shown him.

''Fair enough. I'll help you look for another place tomorrow. Do you want to buy or rent?''

''Rent,'' he said quickly. ''For now.'' He'd spent enough time in Dallas to know he didn't want to live in the city permanently.

Dorian crawled down the couch on her hands and knees and kissed him lightly on the cheek. ''Thank you.''

''For what?''

''For being Brindon. And for believing I might be Dori.''

He smiled and kissed the tip of her nose. ''You're welcome.'' When he'd met her, he had assumed her aloof confidence came from having everything she wanted. Now he knew her self-assurance was an act she'd adopted to hide the fact she didn't have *anything* she wanted.

They had come to a fork in the road. They could have gone their separate ways and never discovered what might have been. If they stayed on the same path a little longer, who knew where they might end up?

Dorian began questioning the possibility of charmed intervention when she experienced another stroke of good luck almost too good to be true. She struck up a conversation with a fellow tenant in the elevator the next day. The man, a successful local interior designer, was about to embark on an unexpected monthlong European buying trip. When she asked who would be looking after his apartment in his absence, he admitted he'd hoped to sublet for security reasons, but didn't think he could find anyone reliable on short notice or for such a short term.

Dorian worked her magic again, and within days Brindon and Reba were installed in the spacious second-floor apartment. She had to do some fast-talking to convince the designer to let Brindon keep his dog, but he had eventually come around when Dorian pointed out the advantages of having a trained former police dog in residence to guard his valuable collection of antiques. She was careful not to let him get a good look at Reba before he left.

With Brindon gone, her place seemed empty. The loneliness gave her incentive to initiate her own self-improvement plan. Brindon made her want to overcome the influences of the past and truly change. Until she did, they didn't have a chance to be happy. She refused to make him as miserable as her mother had made her father.

She had six weeks before their contract ran out. Six weeks to turn her life around. Because if she didn't, she would step aside and let Brindon get on with his. He deserved his happy ending, whether she was part of it or not.

They continued to meet every morning for lessons, but Brindon spent most afternoons on the computer they'd moved downstairs. When she asked what he was working on so diligently, he said he was researching charitable organizations, but offered few details.

Once he felt comfortable with the social skills he'd learned, Dorian arranged social activities to put them to practical use. She called them "midterm exams." They attended a whirl of wine tastings, poetry readings, orchestra concerts and gallery crawls. She dragged him to fashion shows and told him more than he ever wanted to know about haute couture, Dallas-style. He tagged along with her to Art League luncheons where he surprised her by winning over a coterie of hard-line, old-money socialites.

She introduced him to the people he needed to know, powerful people in the inner circles of society. People with connections and clout. But she did not have the power to turn those introductions into alliances. Brindon did that with his straight talk and no-frills attitude. She had taught him many things, but the curriculum had not covered winning friends and influencing people. He knew instinctively how to do that and could work a room without even trying.

The wealthiest, most powerful people gravitated to him, perhaps because he was neither impressed by their wealth nor intimidated by their power. His unspoken message was unmistakably clear.

You can trust me.

Over the next couple of weeks, Dorian introduced him to many of her friends. To their credit, the spoiled debutantes and blasé scions seemed to recognize him for what he was. She had thought those in her circle incapable of appreciating him, but obviously, she hadn't given them enough credit. She'd been concerned he wouldn't fit in, or if he did, they would corrupt him.

Had she actually worried he would pick up their bad habits and haughty ways? The first thing she needed to learn was to stop underestimating her student.

The change was slow and gradual, maybe unnoticeable to anyone except Dorian. But she saw her friends begin to grow in small, significant ways. She observed them being more respectful to themselves and each other. She watched them treat harried clerks and busy waiters a bit more kindly. A couple of the less depraved even developed a social conscience and openly admitted to having interests and causes outside themselves.

Brindon charmed the women without trying, but because he was so obviously a man's man, also won the respect of her most dissolute and self-serving male friends as well. She no longer had to worry about her pupil—he would be successful in whatever he chose to do.

Now that he required less of her time, Dorian began focusing on her own self-improvement program. Maybe she was indeed sand, but if Brindon could be the clay that held her together, she might yet become a better person.

Late one morning, Dorian knocked on the door of the apartment downstairs. She told Brindon to change into work clothes because she had a special activity planned. When he started to climb into the driver's seat of his SUV, she snatched the keys from his hand.

"I'll drive." She climbed behind the wheel and steered the big vehicle through lunch hour traffic.

"Where are we going?"

"I arranged for us to help build a house." She slanted a glance in his direction and was gratified when his mouth dropped open.

"What?"

"With all your research into charities, surely you've heard of Habitat for Humanity?"

"Yes. Volunteers build homes for deserving people who could not otherwise afford one. In return they help build houses for others." He had obviously done his homework on charitable organizations.

"That's right. I thought you might be getting tired of lunching and golfing and counting your money. Living fluffy, I believe you call it?"

"So you volunteered me to build a house?"

"No."

"But I thought—"

"I volunteered both of us. Of course, I don't have a clue what to do, but the project coordinator assured me inexperience didn't matter. He said he'd give me a quickie construction lesson when we get there."

Brindon's face creased in a wide smile. "You came up with this all on your own?"

"I have good ideas, too, you know." She tried to sound miffed, but failed. She was pleased with herself and didn't care if her pleasure showed. Brindon didn't know what she'd been up to, she planned to surprise him. Today was just the latest in a series of happy coincidences that had shown her the good that could come of thinking of others.

A couple of weeks earlier, she had gone through her closets, then talked Tiggy and several other friends into doing likewise. She'd taken several boxes of clothing to Mrs. Treadwell to distribute at the women's shelters for the women to wear to job interviews. While she was there, the director of The Children's Development Fund had convinced her to teach art to a group of school-age children. She'd had a wonderful time, and the kids had seemed to enjoy her lessons. The hugs they'd given her before she left had made her throat tighten with emotion.

Her experience had inspired her to contact Justin Green, the young man who'd helped Brindon become computer literate. He helped her adapt the art history program she'd devised to introduce youngsters at a homeless shelter to the world of fine art. After the class one of the boys told her his family was getting a new house.

And that's where they were going. To help with the construction.

"You do realize you could break a nail today?" Brindon teased.

Fanning the fingers clutching the steering wheel, Dorian grimaced as she examined her perfect French manicure. "I'm willing to make the sacrifice for a good cause."

Two hours later Briny hammered up drywall in the small two-bedroom house under construction and kept a close eye on Dorian. She followed along after him, applying joint compound to the seams for the guy behind her to tape. Briny wasn't keeping her under surveillance because he doubted her efforts. During the course of the long, hot day she had proven a hard worker. She'd listened carefully as the drywall supervisor explained the task, then focused on her work with the same intense concentration she would lavish on a symphony orchestra performance. She didn't complain about the heat and was openly grateful when the refreshment crew came by with drinks and snacks.

She didn't need supervision. Briny watched her because he liked looking at her. She'd tied a scarf over her hair. Snug-fitting jeans molded her willowy legs and hugged her small bottom when she bent to load her taping blade with compound before spreading it over the drywall seams. She smoothed the mixture down the seam, and her breasts moved sensuously under her plain white T-shirt. She was tall and needed only a simple step stool to reach up to the ceiling. Maybe that's why she'd been assigned the task.

She must have felt him watching her because she turned to smile in his direction. He pulled a handkerchief from his back pocket and dabbed a smear of taping compound off her nose.

"Thanks." She tucked a loose strand of hair under her scarf.

"You're welcome."

Their gazes locked for a long moment and his choice was clear. He had to either kiss her or go outside and hose himself down. He swooped in for a quick peck, but when the water lady came by with a rolling ice chest full of cold drinks, they jumped apart like two kids caught necking under the bleachers. Dorian blushed, something he had never seen her do before, and ducked back to work. He mouthed the word *later* so none of their co-workers could hear, and whistled happily as he resumed nailing up drywall. He liked knowing there would be a later.

That evening they were too tired to cook. They went to their apartments to clean up after their exhausting day, then met later at Dorian's to eat the pizza they'd ordered.

"So how do you feel?" Brindon selected an overlarge slice of the deep-dish pepperoni pie.

"Good. Tired." Dorian pulled off a stringy section of cheese, tipped back her head and dropped the hot goo into her mouth. All that physical activity had worked up an appetite such as she'd never known. "Hungry."

"Wait until tomorrow," he warned. "You'll have sore muscles where you didn't even know you had muscles."

"Oh, I'm already achy," she assured him. "But it's a good kind of ache."

He nodded. "I've always done manual work. When they promoted me to foreman on the rig a couple of years ago, it was hard to get used to my new duties. I like working with my hands, really putting my back into the job, so spending so much time driving from location to location, filling out paperwork, checking on the men, took some adjustment.''

"The family we built the house for certainly looked happy. The wife told me they never owned a home before and had actually been living in their car.''

"A lot of people in the world are barely scraping by,'' he said. "When I think about that, I have to wonder why I was singled out to receive such a gift.''

"You still don't believe that was just luck?'' Her tone was teasing, but she really wanted to know.

"No man is entitled to that much luck.'' He took a sip of iced tea. "I've been thinking about what I want to do with the money.''

"And?''

"I'll let you know when I figure out the details.'' He grinned. "Being rich is complicated. I've never had to deal with such large numbers before. Back in Slapdown, I barely made my wages last from one payday to the next.''

"I'm curious. How did that town get its name, anyway?''

He laughed. "Legend has it that a Lebanese peddler was one of the first merchants to arrive in the area. He had a big wagon of supplies and conducted business across a counter made of a board laid across two barrels. When folks came to make a purchase, he would say, 'Slap down your money.' Before long, going to slap down became synonymous with going to town. Eventually, they made it official.''

She smiled. "That's a good story. Tell me more about your town.'' Dorian helped herself to another slice of pizza. She'd never eaten more than two at one sitting in her life.

"There's not much to tell. Main Street is only a few blocks long. There's a couple of gas stations, a grocery store. Post office. A few stores and offices. Whiskey Pete's is a five-stool bar and the only night life in town. More snakes and armadillos than people. Lots of wind and plenty of dust. You can see all the way to the horizon from anyplace in town, with nothing in between but a few steers and oil wells.''

"Where did you live?'' She finished her pizza and wiped her hands on a napkin.

"I rented an old trailer out by the railroad tracks. I'm not kidding when I say 'old.' The floor was falling through in a couple of places. I had to keep nailing plywood over the holes."

She couldn't imagine that. "I'm having a hard time picturing Slapdown."

"You want to see it? Up close and personal?"

"What?"

"I'm planning to drive out and visit my friends and check on some property I'm thinking of buying.

"You want to buy a place in Slapdown?" A knot of apprehension tightened in her stomach at the thought. Not once in the weeks they'd been together had she ever considered that Brindon might want to return to his hometown to live. When she had dared to think of the future, their future, she had assumed he would stay here. In Dallas. With her.

He'd learned to fit into her world. He'd accomplished what he set out to do and could move in the right circles. He'd become the gentleman he wanted to be but was still the man he'd always been. He had a whole other life. One she knew nothing about. One she might never fit into.

"Come with me." He reached across the table and squeezed her hand. "On the way back we can stop by Los Huerfanos, and you can see where I grew up. Meet Mom and Pop Appleton. What do you say?"

She wanted to say no because she was afraid to go. But in the end she said yes, because she was afraid not to.

Chapter Ten

"Are you going to tell me about the property in Slapdown?" Dorian climbed out of the SUV to stretch her legs and leaned against the door while Reba squatted in the heat-burned grass on the side of the road.

"What do you want to know?" Briny retrieved three bottles of cold water from the Navigator's built-in cooler. He handed her one, poured another into a plastic bowl on the ground for Reba, then swigged down the third.

The day had already been hot when they left Dallas a couple of hours ago. The sun had since climbed into the pale, cloudless sky, edging the temperature into the nineties. In west Texas, the last days of August were scorchers, hell on man and beast. He splashed a few drops of water on his face and finger combed the dampness through his hair.

Another example of how much things had changed. He'd spent most of his adult life working outside in all kinds of weather, but a few weeks of living in climate-controlled comfort had spoiled him. He had also spent most of his adult life alone, and those same weeks with Dorian had made him realize he didn't want to live without her.

She punched him lightly on the arm. "You can be really obtuse regarding subtle hints, you know."

"Obtuse?" He playfully tapped his temple as though trying to shake loose the definition. "Oh, yes. Lacking in quickness of intellect, right?"

"Right. The word can also mean insensitive." She pretended to pout. "What do I have to do? Beg you to tell me?"

"You could try. You might bat your eyelashes and throw in a 'pretty please' or two." He'd tried to provoke her curiosity with his silence on the subject, but she'd been reserved this morning, refusing to take the bait until now. "What do you want to know, Dori?"

She didn't answer at first. Shading her eyes, she peered through her designer sunglasses and scanned the flat, brown, empty landscape. "I guess what I'd like to know is, are you planning to buy a home out here? Do you want to move back to west Texas?"

"Would you care?" Care about something, dammit, he urged silently. Care about me. About us.

"I was just curious." She sipped her water and shrugged one shoulder as though his answer were of no real interest.

"You'll find out soon enough. We're almost there." He propped one arm on the car behind her, leaned close and touched his finger to a stray drop of water at the corner of her mouth. He drew his moist fingertip in a lazy line across her tense lower lip. "I'm planning a surprise."

"It has been my experience that not all surprises are pleasant."

She turned away and scooped up Reba's empty water dish before his lips could trace the path his finger had made. "The sun is hot out here." She fanned her face with her hand, as though the action would rid her of curiosity, as well. "Can we go?"

Back on the road, they lapsed into uncomfortable silence. Alan Jackson's plaintive vocals provided a musical counterpoint to the strained mood that sprang up between them. Dorian had tried to make her interest in his plans sound casual, but Briny suspected what she didn't say was more telling than her words. Strong willed and deeply entrenched in the habit of denying her feelings, she would fight their attraction with skilled, evasive tactics. He'd hoped the enforced closeness of this trip would provide the opportunity to talk openly about the future and the possibility they might spend it together.

So far no luck.

He wanted her to be part of his life. He knew that as surely as he knew dawn followed night. His runaway fantasies had galloped past courtship without even slowing and were bearing down hard on marriage. But before he could seriously entertain such thoughts, he needed some encouragement, a sign, no matter how small or grudgingly given. Every time he tried to discuss their relationship, she ducked the subject like a poorly thrown punch.

In the weeks since the night they danced and kissed while Tony Bennett serenaded in the background, she had kept busy, leaving him on his own for long stretches of time. When he asked about her activities, she wouldn't offer details and summed them up as "just some little projects of mine."

He hated every minute they were apart. He lived for every second they spent together. When she wasn't with him, part of him was missing. He could not wait to see her face, hear her voice, touch her skin. She invaded his waking thoughts, haunted his dreams at night.

If that wasn't love, he didn't know what love was. He'd listened to enough sad country-western love songs to recognize the symptoms. Maybe what he'd first felt for Dorian had been worshipful infatuation, an impossible longing for a beautiful, perfect woman he couldn't have.

But he had learned things she never meant to teach.

He'd discovered she was far from perfect. She had fears and secrets, flaws and problems, just like every human ever born. She'd spent a lifetime trying to convince herself she didn't need anyone, but she could not make the delusion true. In the course of his own makeover, he'd learned that appearances were deceiving. Outward beauty was a dubious thing, dependent on the perceptions of others. It could be slipped on and off like a suit of clothes, hidden behind, like a mask.

Inner beauty was a gift and could not be manipulated or denied. Dorian had the potential to be so much more than she ever believed she could be, and Briny wanted to be there when she made the discovery. He wanted to walk beside her every step of the journey.

Like a pet bobcat, his decision to give her time and space to find herself had become damned hard to live with. The terms of their contract were about to expire. Time was running out. He was determined to reveal his feelings sometime during this trip.

Even if telling the truth meant losing her forever.

Brindon stopped by the office of Slapdown's only real estate agent and picked up the key to the mystery property. He drove through the little town's business district, which consisted of a few retail stores and professional buildings. The drive didn't take long. As promised, Main Street was only four blocks long.

Nothing much moved, not even a breeze to relieve the oppressive heat. Slapdown wasn't a place where people hurried. There weren't that many places to go. Dorian watched a small black dog amble down an alley and a trio of shirtless brown-skinned young boys lazily pedal bicycles down the sidewalk.

A few parked cars angled into spaces along the wide main street. She assumed the drivers were conducting business in the stores, but she couldn't be sure. It was possible all the inhabitants had been beamed aboard a recently departed spaceship. They passed the town square. An American flag hung limply from a pole, and hundred-year-old oak trees provided a respite of shade. An elderly man sat on a bench under one of the towering giants and fanned himself with his hat.

"There's old Herb Finnerman," Brindon said as they drove past. "I swear he was sitting in that same spot when I left."

"Slapdown isn't exactly a bustling metropolis, is it?" she asked.

"Nope. If you want excitement, you have to drive up to Midland. There's the Bag and Wag." He indicated a small grocery store on the corner. There were placards advertising

weekly specials in the windows and two gas pumps out front.
"That's where I bought the lottery ticket."

"*The* lottery ticket?"

He nodded. "For years, as regular as clockwork, I went into
the store every payday and bought the same three things: a six
pack, a pizza and a ten-dollar lottery ticket. I guess you could
call it a ritual."

"How many times did you win?"

"Just that once." He glanced at her, his blue eyes as warm
as the west Texas sky. "But when you pick right, one is all
you need."

"Yes, I suppose it is." She wanted to be the right one for
him.

Reba had slept during most of the trip, but she suddenly
perked up as if sensing familiar surroundings. Brindon hit the
automatic window control, and the right side back glass slid
down. The old hound stuck her nose out the window and
barked joyfully to announce her homecoming.

"I think Reba recognizes the place," Dorian said.

Brindon glanced at his dog in the rearview mirror and
grinned. "She's glad to be back. I promised the owners of the
Bag and Wag that if I struck it rich, I'd use the money to do
something good."

"Doesn't the vendor who sells the winning ticket receive a
large sum?"

Brindon nodded. "It's really strange how things worked
out. The Smiths were worried they'd have to go out of business. Ben's cataracts were getting bad, and Elda couldn't run
the place by herself since she was taking care of their two
great-grandkids while their granddaughter cooked part-time
over at the café. But with the chunk of change they got for
selling me the winning ticket, Ben was able to have cataract
surgery, they paid off the store's mortgage, and they helped
their granddaughter get back on her feet. Now they're all—"

"Living happily ever after?" Dorian put in with a smile.

"Yeah." He grinned. "Come to think of it, they are."

"So you've kept up with your friends while you were in
Dallas?"

"I like to stay current on what's happening." He waved to a middle-aged woman sweeping the sidewalk in front of an antique store. The woman's face lit up in recognition, and her hand flapped in greeting. "That's Connie Birdsong. She's been trying for years to get area antique dealers interested in renting the empty storefronts. She thinks if Slapdown becomes an antique hunters' mecca, it will draw more business to town."

He pointed across the street to where a man was putting the finishing touches on a sign that spelled Avalon Antiques across a wide expanse of glass. "Looks like she's finally making some progress. Business in the downtown stores has picked up since the Smiths' granddaughter, Mary Sue Biggs, started cooking full-time at the café. In fact, revenues all over town have increased during the last quarter."

"Really?"

"Yep. The town council is reconsidering building a community health clinic. The project had been in the works for a long time, but plans were tabled last year due to lack of funds." Brindon braked at a stop sign. "If Slapdown had a doctor, folks wouldn't have to drive so far for medical care. More young people would stay instead of migrating out. Keeping the new generation is the best way to ensure a small town's growth and prosperity."

"Amazing."

"What is?"

"Brindon Tucker wins the lottery and the whole darn town benefits."

He considered her words for a moment. "I think you may be on to something there." His eyes widened with comprehension. "Say, do you think that's the plan?"

Dorian didn't know what to think. Her cynical tendency was not to believe in such things as fate and predestination. But Brindon clearly felt a part of the Slapdown community. Like a chameleon, he'd adapted and fit so readily into her world she hadn't considered he might maintain ties with his past life.

At the edge of town, he pointed out a long, low building in the middle of a dusty gravel parking lot. "That's where everyone's gathering later. I told you about Whiskey Pete's, didn't I?''

"The only night life in town, I believe you said."

"That's right. Remind me to teach you some country line dances. Some of the boys will bring their guitars, and their ladies will supply the food. Pete will provide the beer and cook the barbecue. I guarantee, you have never tasted anything as good as Pete's barbecue. You'll think you've died and gone to heaven."

Good. Because what she'd seen of Slapdown so far was more reminiscent of the other place, much farther south. "All your friends are turning out for the big Welcome Home Brindon party?"

"No one calls me that except you," he reminded her with a grin. "Around here, folks don't need an excuse to celebrate or throw a party. They just like to get together and have a good time."

As Dorian watched the scenery unfold on the other side of the SUV's tinted windows, she felt she'd been transported, if not to purgatory, then to another planet. She had lived in the state all her life and knew how hot and dry summers could be. But this was an unfamiliar Texas, one that was a long way from the stately homes and carefully manicured, heavily irrigated lawns of Dallas's most exclusive neighborhoods.

The residents of Slapdown were obviously a thrifty lot, unwilling to waste a precious commodity like water on anything as unimportant as landscaping. The brown grass was parched, the wilted petunias and zinnias in front of the modest houses faded. In small backyard gardens, straggling tomato plants and sprawling squash vines barely clung to life. Everything in town was lightly coated with pervasive gray dust.

Granny Pru called it Texas talcum powder.

They drove another mile or so before Brindon turned the SUV into a dirt driveway winding up to a white-sided, green-shuttered mobile home set on a slight rise well back from the road. There was no yard, but someone had recently mowed down the surrounding weeds with a bushhog.

"Here we are," Brindon announced as he parked and switched off the engine.

"*This* is the property you're thinking of buying?" Dorian hadn't intended her question to sound like an accusation, but he had definitely succeeded in surprising her.

"Actually, I'm not thinking of buying the property now," he said.

"That's a relief." She laughed nervously. "You had me worried there for a moment."

"I've definitely decided to buy it. We'll run back by Art Campbell's later, and I'll give him a deposit so he can draw up the papers."

"You wouldn't want anyone to snap this treasure out from under you."

"Come on, let's get in out of the heat." He grabbed their overnight cases and garment bags from the back of the Navigator and led the way up the wooden steps to the tacked-on porch. Fitting the key he'd obtained from the agent into the lock, he pushed open the storm door.

Dorian stepped inside the double-wide kiln, and one-hundred-plus-degree heat slapped her in the face. "I didn't think it was meteorologically possible," she gasped, "but the air is actually cooler outside."

Brindon hurried down the narrow hallway and quickly located the thermostat. He switched on the central air-conditioning, and the system roared to life, releasing a musty odor slightly less pleasant than the predominant scent of moth balls and old bacon grease. "Things will be bearable in a couple of minutes," he promised when he rejoined her.

She looked around, dismayed by the uncomfortable-looking sea-green furniture and worn mauve carpeting. Bearable? She didn't think so. Surely Brindon wasn't seriously considering living here. She'd worked hard to instill in him an appreciation for the finer things of life. Was that old saying, "You can take the boy out of the country, but you can't take the country out of the boy," really true?

He showed her to the master bedroom at the north end of the trailer and deposited her bags on the floor. "Art said his wife put clean sheets on the beds for us.'' He reached up and pulled a chain, setting the ceiling fan blades into motion. Out of balance, they made an annoying whump, whump, whump with each revolution.

"That was nice of her."

"You have your own bathroom in here." He opened the door to prove his point, and she caught a glimpse of gold-veined mirrors and pink ceramic tile. "I'll be in one of the bedrooms on the other end, so yell if you need anything. The utilities have been turned on, so feel free to take a bath or shower if you want, before we head over to the party."

"Thank you." Dorian stood in the dusty, half-empty room, unsure why she was here, so far from everything comfortable and familiar. She thought she'd made progress overcoming her bred-in-the-bone snooty-rich-girl attitude. But she hated this sweat lodge masquerading as a mobile home. Her chest tightened and her throat burned. She might even cry if she could come up with a legitimate excuse to do so. Surely there was a giant dust mote somewhere just waiting to sting her eye.

When in doubt, focus on fashion. "What should I wear tonight?"

Brindon stopped at the door, turned around and shrugged. "It doesn't matter. Whatever you're comfortable in. I'm sure what you brought will be fine."

She hadn't packed anything appropriate for a line-dancing, barbecue-munching, beer-swilling occasion. "I can't go to the party."

"Yes, you can."

"I won't fit in."

"Sure you will."

"I don't belong here."

"Of course you do."

"Your friends will hate me."

"No, they won't."

They should. She hated herself for thinking harshly of the town and people Brindon cared about. For thinking she was too good to live in the hot, smelly trailer. For wanting to run back to Dallas as fast as the four-wheel-drive would take her.

What made her think she could rise above her upbringing and actually demonstrate the acceptance and tolerance and patience Brindon had shown her friends?

She didn't possess his kindly disposition, and she was beginning to suspect compassion was a quality that could not be learned. When they'd been passing out generosity of spirit, she'd been shoving her way to the head of the hypercritical judgmental queue.

"I'm very tired." Thinking about her character flaws exhausted her. "Do I have time to rest before we go?" When fashion fails, take a nap.

Brindon strode to the side of the bed and turned back the blanket, revealing the pale pink sheets beneath. "Sure. I need to go into town for a little while to see some people and take care of a little business. I'll leave Reba here with you. Will you mind being alone?"

"I'll be fine." She could handle a little solitude here in this empty trailer on the ragged edge of nowhere. But what made her want to go to bed and cover up her head was the thought that she might have to spend the rest of her life alone. She unzipped her Dolce & Gabbana tote, looking for her sleep mask. If there was ever a time she needed to block out her surroundings, this was it.

"If you're asleep when I get back, I'll try not to wake you. We don't have to leave for Pete's until six." When he bent and kissed her forehead, the heat of his lips matched the searing Texas sun outside. Before she could move away, she melted like a chocolate bar on a warm day and slumped against him. His strong arms welcomed, encircled, comforted.

Being held made her feel better than she deserved. She'd missed the closeness they had shared the night Brindon's passionate kisses had awakened her desire, and the longings stirred deep within her. She was playing with fire, but she relented for a moment and rested her cheek against his chest.

"Is something wrong?" he whispered.

His breath stirred her hair, pricking her scalp with pleasure. She wanted to feel that tingling pleasure all over. She wanted Brindon. But he came as part of a package, his past and his future was as important to him as the fleeting present. She couldn't take what she wanted while rejecting what she couldn't accept. Even she wasn't that selfish or unfair.

Brindon's hometown made her uncomfortable. From the moment they'd arrived, she had felt like an interloper. An outsider. An impostor. How could she explain to him that being here reminded her of all the differences between them? Differences she'd wrongfully hoped to overcome by doing a little volunteer work. How could she have been so foolish? So blind. "I'm just nervous about meeting your friends."

He tucked a finger under her chin and forced her gaze to meet his own. His blue eyes were alight with the sincerity she'd come to expect from him. "You don't have a thing to worry about, Dori. My friends are going to love you."

Chapter Eleven

Shouts and bear hugs and enthusiastic backslapping greeted Briny as soon as he and Dorian walked into Whiskey Pete's later that evening. Someone thrust a cold bottle of beer into his hand as they were swept into the crowd of well-wishers. He slipped easily back into the hometown rhythms. Despite weeks in the big city and the turn his life had taken, he was made to feel as if he'd never left town.

Men pumped his hand, old ladies kissed his cheek, and a couple of young ones stood on tiptoe to smack him squarely on the lips. Hopefully, the dimmed house lights concealed his sheepish expression and the self-conscious flush that warmed his face.

When he'd accepted his friends' invitation, he hadn't expected to be treated like a conquering hero. He didn't want his homecoming to overshadow the announcement the mayor would make later tonight. His return to Slapdown wasn't nearly as significant as that of the real guest of honor.

Briny hardly had time to think. Questions and comments flew out of the crowd so fast, he couldn't begin to figure out who said what.

"You look different, man. What happened to the mustache?"

"Gosh, Briny, we didn't know you were so good-looking."

"We thought you'd forgotten all about your old friends, Briny."

"How's Dallas been treating you, buddy?"

"We sure miss you out on the rig."

"Reckon you'll ever come back to work?"

"Have you run through your winnings yet?"

"How long you planning to stay this time?"

Briny did his best to respond to everyone who approached him, while keeping Dorian close in an effort to reassure her. Tall, beautiful and model slim, she stood stiffly at his side, apparently unruffled by the men's openly appreciative looks and the women's appraising glances. They would be hard-pressed to find fault with her polished appearance, but he knew it was human nature to try. The viselike grip with which she held his hand was the only outward indication of her stress and told him she knew she was being evaluated.

Normally hospitable toward strangers, the citizens of Slapdown treated Dorian as warmly as they would any newcomer. That is until Briny finally got around to introducing her.

"Hey, everyone." It took a few moments to gain the noisy crowd's attention, and a few more for the friendly banter to quiet down enough for him to speak. "I want you all to meet a special friend of mine, who has been showing me around Dallas and introducing me to folks there. Say hello to Dorian Burrell."

The name echoed through the crowd like an icy wind, and its effect was immediate. Briny hadn't felt a room cool off so fast since the last blue norther had roared into town. The tide of people ebbed. Laughter broke off in mid-guffaw. Some murmured a polite "How do you do?" or "Pleased to meet you," before drifting toward the bar for another round. Others excused themselves before lighting out for the buffet table. Someone dropped coins into the jukebox, and an old Hank Williams song lured a few couples onto the dance floor.

Before long Briny and Dorian were left standing all alone

under an advertiser's wall clock whose face was a rushing waterfall of beer.

"That's what you get for bringing Typhoid Mary to the party." Dorian pressed her elbow against his ribs for emphasis. She was too smart not to realize what had happened; he was too sensitive not to be embarrassed. His friends hadn't meant to be rude, but Dorian had found their reaction as mortifying as an intentional reproach.

"I didn't see that coming," he said by way of apology. "I shouldn't have sprung you on them like that."

"I told you not all surprises were pleasant." She shifted, balancing her weight on four-inch heels, but her expression did not change. He saw the hurt in her eyes, even though her outward expression never changed. She was trying hard not to let on how much the snub had hurt her. Fighting to keep up appearances.

"It'll be all right." Briny squeezed her hand. "The name just startled them, that's all."

Country folks were as conscious of lineage as Old World aristocrats. They used it to establish a newcomer's ties to the community. Formal calling cards were unheard of, but being Mr. So and So's nephew or Mrs. Whatchacallit's cousin on her daddy's side had eased many a stranger into rural society. Dorian's prominent family, while familiar to local cliques, had never been part of them.

"Yes, we've been known to strike terror into the hearts of our fellow Texans," she said tightly. "There's a saying almost as famous as 'Remember the Alamo!'"

"What's that?"

"'Run! Here comes a Burrell!'"

His laughter didn't get past her wall of reserve. "Oh, they'll come around. Give them time."

"I should live so long," she murmured.

"What?" A wave of music from the jukebox rolled over her words, and he wasn't sure he caught her meaning. Before he could ask questions, Connie Birdsong invited them to help themselves to the food. Briny looked longingly at the long table pushed up against the back wall. Covered by a red-checked tablecloth, it was laden with a mouthwatering array of savory dishes. He leaned down and spoke into Dorian's ear. "Would you like something to eat?"

"No, thank you." She lifted her chin and tucked her little red purse under her arm. "I'm not hungry."

"We haven't eaten since eleven o'clock this morning," he reminded her. "Why don't you have something?"

"How about a Manhattan?"

"Sorry. They don't serve hard liquor here. Only beer."

"The place is called Whiskey Pete's."

"I know. Long story. Bottle or draft?"

"I don't like beer."

"How about a soft drink?"

"Never mind. I don't want anything."

"Are you sure?" Briny tried to tempt her by bragging about Pete's secret barbecue sauce, but Dorian wasn't interested. At the first hint of trouble, she had moved back into denial mode. She wasn't hungry. She wasn't thirsty. She didn't care.

This was not how he'd planned the evening to go.

"You go ahead." She stood her ground, proud and unflappable in the face of the unintended slight. "I'll be fine."

Not knowing what else to do, Briny made his way down the table. He traded jokes with some of the men he'd worked with on the oil rig while he heaped a heavy-duty paper plate with barbecued beef, potato salad and baked beans. He glanced up from a large bowl of coleslaw, and his gut twisted at the sight of Dorian standing silent and alone.

She could no more take part in the activity flowing around her than a polished stone could become part of the river.

Briny sighed. This was a setback he hadn't anticipated. He wasn't mad at his friends. Their reaction was understandable. They hadn't given Dorian the cold shoulder because they mistrusted or disliked Burrells; in the years he'd worked for Chaco Oil, he'd never heard a disparaging word spoken against any of the company's past or current owners. But Dorian was the only heir of Prudence Burrell, the woman who controlled the company for which many of the people in Slapdown worked.

In a way their fates were controlled by Burrells, and that gave Dorian power that could be wielded for good or bad as she saw fit. The invisible line separating her from everyone in Slapdown was as widely acknowledged and carefully observed as the one dividing European royalty and commoners.

Dorian's presence put a damper on the festivities and made everyone uncomfortable. They tried to be polite. They just didn't know how to act around her, and she wasn't making it easy for them. She had donned her glamour armor again tonight, probably because she felt safe behind her flawless makeup and carefully styled hair. He knew she hadn't deliberately tried to set herself apart from every other person in the room. She just couldn't help it. The princess did not know how to mingle with common folk.

Her perfume was so subtle no one else in the room would realize it had been custom formulated for her body chemistry. But since they all had noses, they *would* probably figure out she didn't buy it by the quart at the local discount center. Her unpretentious jewelry was tasteful and understated, yet the least discriminating roughneck in the crowd would know the diamonds dangling from her ears and wrist were real.

Dammit! When she asked him what she should wear tonight, he should have explained that Slapdown casual was a far cry from the casual she was used to. But he couldn't have talked coherently, even if he'd known what to say, because when she stepped out of her room at the trailer she had stolen his breath away.

She was a knockout in the lacy, red, form-hugging, knee-length skirt, her soft neck and shoulders bared by a creamy white top. Even her shoes were sexy—red high-heeled sandals with narrow straps that tied around her slim ankles.

She'd looked so perfect, he hadn't had the heart to suggest she change into something more suitable for the occasion. He glanced around and noticed most of the women present were dressed in T-shirts and blue jeans or denim skirts. Some of the older ladies wore pastel pantsuits with flower-print blouses.

Dorian appeared as out of place as a brightly plumed parrot in a room full of mud hens.

He tensed when he caught the assessing glances the women angled in her direction. She felt them, too, he could tell. But she would never let anyone know how miserable she was. She hid the fact she was vulnerable to censure, defenseless against pain. How often had her self-protective facade been mistaken for haughtiness?

Briny could hardly blame anyone for misunderstanding. Insecure about his own place in the social hierarchy, he'd felt stumble-footed and tongue-tied the first time he'd met Dorian. If he hadn't carried a million-dollar passport, he never would have gotten to know her, because she would not have allowed him to enter her inner circle.

She wouldn't have dared to take the chance.

Not because she felt superior to him, as he'd once believed. But because she felt inferior to everyone. That's why she kept her distance. And it was why she continued to fight their powerful attraction.

Realization struck like summer lightning. Damn! The idea that Dorian Burrell believed she wasn't good enough for Briny Tucker was a startling revelation and one that he could not contemplate on an empty stomach. Filled with a startling insight that put all the other knowledge he'd gained to shame, Briny leaned against the wall and devoured the food on his plate while mulling over the implications of his discovery.

Dorian longed for a charm that would magically whisk her back to Dallas. She much preferred mingling with boring people at some meaningless social event to standing here, a well-dressed reminder of Brindon's biggest mistake. It was easier to fit in with people she didn't care about. These men and women were Brindon's friends, their opinions mattered to him. And therefore they mattered to her. She wanted their approval and had come here hoping she'd changed enough and they would recognize her efforts to become a better person. Hoping they would like her.

But that hadn't happened. Despite her efforts, the reaction of the citizens of Slapdown indicated Dorian Burrell was not a likable person.

First of all, she was dressed all wrong. She realized her mistake as soon as she walked in the door. When she was packing for the trip, she had thought the red lace skirt and white jersey peasant blouse with long, poufy sleeves would be just the thing for a party in a place called Whiskey Pete's. The designer had marketed it as casual country attire. What a joke! She couldn't believe she was stupid enough to think an outfit that cost over eight hundred dollars would fulfill the dress code here.

No wonder everyone hated her.

Where was Brindon? Why didn't he come to her rescue? Her stomach knotted, and she searched the room until she found him, standing head and shoulders above the group of earnest-looking men who had cornered him near the buffet table. His eyes met hers. He winked and shrugged as though apologizing for his popularity.

At least he had something to eat. She was starving. And the home-cooked food smelled delicious. But she couldn't eat because she was filled with the sick feeling that her happy fantasy was about to end. Ignoring her rumbling stomach and willing it into submission was good practice while she waited. If she had to start denying her needs again, she might as well start with food.

She noticed a small group of musicians setting up amplifiers and mikes on a raised dais on one side of the dimly lit tavern. She watched them for a moment before turning her attention to the people clustered in booths and at candlelit tables. Laughter floated around her. She watched lips curve into smiles. Heard the sound of their carefree banter. They were strangers to her. But she wanted their acceptance.

The irony was not lost on her. In a stroke of karmic justice, the name that had long opened doors in her world had slammed them shut in Briny's. For most of her life she hadn't had to do anything. Just being Dorian Burrell was endorsement enough. Here, being a Burrell was an obstacle to overcome.

Was she up to the task?

She had to try. These were Brindon's friends. She didn't want them to find her lacking. How could she be part of his life if she turned her back on the people who cared about him? Sucking up a deep, steadying breath, Dorian clutched her evening bag and approached a small knot of gaily chattering women gathered near the end of the bar. They went solemn and silent at her approach.

"Hello," she tried.

"Hi." They spoke in unison like a Greek chorus.

"Lovely party."

"Yeah."

"I like the decorations." The gingham tablecloths and candles were a nice touch.

"Right."

They fidgeted in uncomfortable silence until one of the younger women mentioned a problem she was having potty training her toddler. The older ladies offered encouragement and advice, but Dorian could only nod and smile. Clearly she had nothing to offer on that subject.

She stood quietly as the group discussed the weather, the new kindergarten teacher and the sale at Yerley's Department Store. Finally, someone brought up the topic of food. Safe enough. Thinking she could actually contribute something to the discussion, Dorian jumped in.

"My sous chef gave me some wonderful light pasta recipes. I'd be happy to share them sometime."

The women exchanged puzzled looks. "A sous what?" someone asked.

"Chef. *Sous* means 'under' in French. A sous chef is an assistant."

"You actually have a chef?" one lady asked with ill-concealed envy.

"Oh, no. Not full-time. Brindon and I hired one to give us cooking lessons."

"You and who?"

"Brindon?" The name didn't seem to ring a bell. "Briny," Dorian clarified.

"You're telling us Briny Tucker took cooking lessons from a French chef?"

"That's right."

"Our Briny?"

"Yes." Why was that so hard to believe?

"I'd like to see that." The women tittered.

Dorian didn't know what to make of their behavior. Had she said something wrong?

A pretty young redhead in a short, skintight T-shirt and hip-baring blue jeans laughed. "That's pretty funny. Considering."

"Considering what?" Self-improvement wasn't a laughing matter to Dorian, but she would try to be cordial. If it killed her.

"Considering how the man eats peanut butter and maple syrup for breakfast." The other women giggled at the implication in the redhead's words.

The knot in Dorian's stomach morphed into a tangled mass of misgiving. The young woman's intimate knowledge of Brindon's favorite breakfast food was just one more reminder that while Dorian played no role in his past, these people did. What made her think she could be part of his future?

The lady she'd seen sweeping in front of the antique store spoke up in an obvious effort to ease the tension. "What is it you do for a living, Miss Burrell?"

"Please call me Dorian." What did she do for a living? Up until June she hadn't done a damned thing. These women probably scrimped and saved and worked hard to make ends meet. What would they think if they knew she lunched and shopped and golfed while waiting for trust fund deposits?

But she did have a job, she realized. At least until her contract with Brindon expired. "I'm an image consultant." Surely that occupation was more acceptable than ex-debutante heiress.

"And you're working for Briny?" asked the woman he'd introduced as Elda Smith, one half of the Bag and Wag proprietorship.

"At the moment, yes."

"What is it you do for him exactly?" The antique lady's curiosity seemed genuine.

"I've been teaching him…proper etiquette. And I…show

him how to project the right public image. How to dress…and behave.''

The explanation sounded lame, even to Dorian, and was met by an exchange of frosty looks among the women. ''What's wrong with the way Briny acts?'' Elda asked suspiciously. ''He's a good man. We're all mighty fond of him just the way he is.''

''Of course…it's just that he hired me to…widen his horizons.''

''Uh-hmm.'' The redhead's speculative gaze swept Dorian from her barely-there sandals to her diamond earrings and suggested that he had hired her for other things. She glanced knowingly at the others, who poked one another in the ribs. ''Is that what they're calling it these days?''

Dorian looked around desperately for a way to escape this uncomfortable and humiliating situation. There was never a magic carpet around when she needed one, but if she didn't move away soon, she would have to stoop to justifying her existence to these women. Within her own circle, she could trade barbs and give as good as she got in the witty repartee department. She was lost among women who obviously thought she was some highly paid lascivious socialite who had taken unfair advantage of their favorite millionaire oil rig foreman.

She half expected them to form rank around him like a phalanx of presidential bodyguards and whisk him away from her evil clutches. She had tried to make nice, but the Slapdown Ladies' Inquisition League was having none of it.

The redhead gave Dorian one last critical look. ''Adoo!''

''I beg your pardon?'' Dorian wasn't sure whether the sound was a word or a sneeze.

''Adoo? That's French for I'm outta here!'' The redhead turned with a flounce and disappeared into the crowd.

Before Dorian could say something she'd regret later, the band struck up a slow country tune, and Briny appeared at her side. ''Hey, teach, don't you owe me a dance?''

Dorian went weak with relief. *Get me out of here before I have to scratch eyes and pull out hair.* ''Yes, I believe I do.''

She smiled graciously at the Briny Bodyguard Brigade as she stepped into the protective circle of his arms.

"Dori taught me everything I know about waltzing," he told the women. "When we're done, I'd be happy to give any one of you ladies a turn around the floor to demonstrate my skill." He smiled down at Dorian. "Teacher says I need the practice."

They excused themselves from the group, and the women's heads bent together in animated discussion, thankfully pitched too low for her to hear.

"They hate me," she said.

"They don't know you," he protested.

"That's right. If they knew me, they'd be heating tar and plucking feathers."

"You're imagining things." He led her around the small dance floor. "That's a real nice bunch of ladies."

"That's what they said about Lizzie Borden, Ma Barker and Lady Macbeth."

"Is that your stomach I hear growling louder than the Sagebrush Brotherhood can play?" he teased.

"I told you I'm not hungry."

"Liar." Brindon tugged her close, and she tucked her head under his chin. When he spoke, his tone was exaggerated and sensual. "That barbecue is warm and tender and juicy. It practically melts in your mouth."

"I don't want to hear about it."

"And the potato salad?" He moaned in mock ecstasy. "A subtle medley of sweet and tart flavors. Rich-bodied with mayonnaise, yet piquant with a hint of mustard."

"Piquant?" Dorian snorted. "Do you even know what piquant means?"

"It means provocative," he said in a low, wolfish tone. "Agreeably stimulating to the palate." His breath teased her skin, just as his words teased her imagination.

"You are so full of it, your eyes should be brown."

"Come on, Dori. You want it. You know you do." He nibbled her neck and the warm caress of his lips sent an avalanche of desire rumbling through her.

"Shut up!" How could she be amused and turned on at the same time? Brindon was the only man who'd ever had that effect on her.

"You don't know what you're missing. Don't hold back. Give yourself to the moment. Let go your inhibitions. Stop denying what you want. What you need." He two-stepped her in the direction of the buffet table. When they arrived, they stopped dancing long enough for him to scoop up a paper plate and load it with food. He offered the plate, but when she reached for it, he pulled back.

"I've got what you want, baby," he said in a suggestive growl. "But I'm gonna make you beg for it."

She laughed at his antics. Evidently he had mastered the double entendre when she wasn't looking. "In your dreams." She glanced around. Several people were watching them. She didn't care.

"That's where you live. In my dreams. C'mon. Tell me how much you want it." He passed the plate of barbecue under her nose.

"Give me that!" Dorian snatched the food from his hands and dug in hungrily. Denial just didn't seem necessary when Brindon was around. She ignored the titillating sound of his husky laughter.

"See, I always know what you like."

"Yeah, potato salad!"

They both looked up when the front door opened and a latecomer stepped into the tavern. Even from across the room, with lights dimmed and candles flickering, Dorian recognized a face she hadn't seen for years. The last face she had expected to see here. Or anywhere, for that matter. Startled and panic-stricken, she stopped chewing and stared at the new arrival to confirm her suspicions.

It couldn't be.

But it was.

Chapter Twelve

"Hey, everybody! Doc's here!" The crowd gravitated to the new arrival, welcoming her with the same warmth they'd shown Brindon. And denied Dorian.

"I was afraid she wouldn't make it tonight." Brindon was obviously happy to see the young woman who was shaking hands and talking animatedly with his friends. "C'mon, I want you to meet—"

"Mallory Peterson." The name slipped out of Dorian on a startled breath. The poor, mousy premed student she had rebuffed so thoughtlessly in the Thorndyke library all those years ago was a ghost from her own past.

Brindon's brows drew down in confusion. "How is it you know Mallory?"

"We went to school together."

"Well, there's a coincidence for the record book."

Dorian dropped her plate into a plastic garbage can. She couldn't eat. Her stomach churned with the sick certainty that Mallory's arrival wasn't a coincidence at all. It was the missing piece in the puzzle she'd been trying to solve since falling under Brindon's spell. "You go ahead and talk to her," she urged. "I'm tired. I'm going to sit down."

Leon Davis, a middle-aged man in a white Western shirt tugged Mallory's hand, and she followed him to the bandstand. He stepped up to the microphone and waved for quiet. "Ladies and gentleman, if I could have your attention, I've got a real important announcement to make."

The crowd settled, found seats.

"As mayor, it's my privilege to welcome Dr. Mallory Peterson home to Slapdown." The room erupted in applause. People whistled and stamped their feet. Clearly, Mallory was as well liked as Brindon.

"Don't be bashful, honey. Step into the limelight," the mayor urged. "You've earned it."

Mallory had changed since the last time Dorian saw her. But most people changed in nine years. She had been studious and serious then. Now she exuded a reassuring air of competence and humility. Dressed in simple white slacks and a pale blue blouse, she stood on the dais next to the mayor, embarrassed by all the attention. Her hair was different than Dorian remembered. In college the thick natural curls had been an unremarkable shade of brown. They were lighter now, a lovely ginger color that illuminated her pretty, peach-pale face.

The room was too dark, and Dorian was too far away to see the color of Mallory Peterson's eyes, but she knew they were light golden brown because she recalled the hurt that had flashed in their depths when Dorian rejected her friendly overtures that day in the library.

"I know everyone remembers Mallory," the mayor said. "She was born and raised here. She earned a full-ride scholarship and graduated from Baylor Medical School. She just finished her residency in family medicine and has come home to start practicing. Give Dr. Peterson a warm west-Texas welcome!"

Mallory smiled and stepped up to the microphone. "I'm glad to be here. I made this town a promise when I left. I promised I would return to take care of the people who encouraged me to realize my dream. You don't know how much your support meant to me."

As another round of applause died down, Mayor Davis

scanned the crowd until he spotted Brindon. "Briny Tucker! Get on up here and tell Mallory your big news."

Brindon stepped onto the dais and gave her a hug. "I remember when this little girl went off to college. Everyone expected big things from her, and she hasn't let us down. Mallory, I'm proud to tell you the town council has approved construction of a community health clinic outside of town."

The crowd clapped and hooted and hollered.

Dorian knew now how important the town was to Brindon. How important he was to the town. He belonged here. But she didn't.

"We've received a federal grant from a program designed to improve rural health care. The government has agreed to match any funds we raise, and ground-breaking on the clinic will begin within the month. We can't offer you many perks, but there's a nice double-wide trailer on the property, and you can live in it rent-free for as long as you want."

Dr. Mallory Peterson dashed a happy, grateful tear from her eye. "I don't know what to say...except thank you."

"Don't thank us yet," Brindon teased. "We're putting you to work."

"Good. That's why I'm here."

Dorian applauded along with everyone else, stiffening her face to hide her emotions. The real reason for Mallory's propitious arrival was obvious. Fate's way of reminding her she would never be accepted in Slapdown. Never fit in like Brindon and Mallory. Dorian was an outsider. An interloper. A Burrell.

Brindon approached the table with the town's new doctor in tow. "Hello, Mallory," Dorian said. "Congratulations."

The doctor's face lit up in pleased recognition, and Dorian recognized the look from that day in the library, when Mallory had thought Dorian might want to be her friend. "Gosh, Dorian, it's been a long time, hasn't it?" Mallory hugged her with such affection, Dorian could almost believe they *were* friends.

"Yes. A very long time. I'm glad to see you accomplished everything you set out to do. You always were determined."

"I was lucky," she demurred.

Her eyes *were* golden brown. They were kind and filled with intelligence. If her own heart ever stopped beating, she would want to see Dr. Peterson's compassionate face on the other side of the defibrillator. "Luck had nothing to do with it. You worked hard. I'm sure you are an excellent physician." Dorian, on the other hand, was excellent at nothing.

"I'm trying. Brindon, you big sweetheart. This clinic was all your doing, wasn't it?"

He shrugged. "Maybe I nudged things along a little."

"Mayor Davis told me you donated the property."

"It's the least I could do."

"And put up the money so the town could get the matching funds."

"I consider it an investment. In the future."

"It's a miracle. Thank you."

"Hey, I'm no miracle worker," he protested. "If you want to thank someone, thank Lady Luck. She's the one who got this ball rolling."

"So will you be staying in Slapdown?" Mallory directed her question to them both, as though she considered them a couple.

Brindon slipped his arm around Dorian's shoulder. "We haven't worked out the kinks in our plans yet. We're heading back to Dallas in the morning. Why don't you stop by early, and I'll show you the trailer and the clinic site."

"I'll do that. I guess it's safe to say this now." Mallory smiled up at Brindon. "You've been my hero for as long as I can remember."

"I have?" The look on his face told Dorian he was genuinely taken aback by Mallory's heartfelt declaration.

"You inspired me by the way you helped people." She turned to Dorian. "I guess you know about his infamous loans."

"Tell me." Give me another nail to drive into the coffin I'll bury my love in.

"Briny's a soft touch. If somebody needed an extra fifty or hundred to get them through to payday, he slipped it to them, no questions asked. When I was in high school, my mom waited tables at the diner. Briny was her favorite customer, always left a five-dollar tip. Even when he ordered a cup of coffee.''

"Hey, your mama was a good waitress."

Mallory opened her purse and removed a crisp bill. "Here. I know you never asked anyone to pay you back, but I want to."

"For what?"

"Don't you remember? The day I left for college, you stopped by the house and gave me a dictionary. You said something in it might come in handy.'' She smiled. "A month later I needed a hundred dollars for a special science lab I wanted to take. The fee wasn't covered by my tuition waiver, and I couldn't ask my folks for it. I had no idea how I was going to come up with the cash.

"Then the day of the registration deadline, I bumped against my desk and the dictionary Briny gave me fell on the floor. When I picked it up, I found a hundred-dollar bill tucked between pages 708 and 709. Do you know which words head the columns on those pages?"

They admitted they did not.

"*Luck*. And *luckier*." She kissed Brindon on the cheek. "Thank you for being my lucky charm. As it turned out, the professor in the science lab was the one who wrote the letter of recommendation that got me into Baylor."

"You're awfully quiet." Brindon glanced at Dorian before returning his attention to the road.

"There's not much to say." They'd left Slapdown after an agonizing breakfast at the diner. Brindon had been congratulated and thanked and openly admired by everyone who came in for eggs and coffee while she had been politely ignored. After a quick stop at Los Huerfanos, they would be on their way back to Dallas.

"What's wrong?" He reached over and turned down the music, a subtle cue for her to start answering the questions she'd evaded all morning. "You've been acting strange since the party last night."

"Strange as in off the medication?" she said with false levity.

"What happened?"

"Nothing."

"Did someone say something to upset you?"

"No." On the contrary, someone had said something that helped her make a difficult decision. She knew now what she had to do. Silence was her way of dealing with the pain.

"So we're square? Everything's all right?"

"Yes," she said quietly. "Everything is finally all right."

He took her at her word and was relieved enough to yodel along with Dwight Yoakum until he embarrassed himself and stopped. Brindon was too trusting. He didn't belong in a world where no one said what they meant and nothing was as it seemed. He belonged in Slapdown where a man's word was his bond. Where promises were kept and dreams came true. Where ordinary people recognized the fakes in their midst and drove them out.

"I still can't get over little Mallory turning out to be a doctor," he said in apparent amazement.

"Was there ever any doubt? As I recall, she was very determined to succeed, even as a teenager."

"You never did say how you two met," he prompted.

She couldn't tell him the truth about the way she'd treated Mallory all those years ago. Or how the shame she'd secretly nurtured had come back to haunt her in the guise of a dedicated young physician. "We met in the library at Thorndyke. She helped me find a book I was looking for."

"It all seems like part of the plan, doesn't it?" He sounded gratified by the hand fate had dealt. "I mean, think about the way one thing has led to the next—like a long line of dominoes falling in a predetermined pattern."

"I hate to argue with your cosmic view of the world, but what you have described could also be called coincidences."

"Coincidences are God's way of remaining anonymous," he said with a quick grin.

"You should put that on a bumper sticker."

"Where do you think I got it?"

"Mallory seemed genuinely pleased with the trailer," she said to change the subject. The young doctor had stopped by that morning. She hadn't smelled the odor of stale grease clinging to the curtains or heard the annoying sound the ceiling fan made. She had looked around enthusiastically and seen the possibilities.

"I think she likes the idea of being close to the clinic." Brindon braked at a crossroads, then steered the SUV onto a two-lane highway. "That way if there's an emergency, she'll be right there. Her coming home to practice is the best thing that ever happened to Slapdown."

"No, that distinction belongs to you." Between them, Brindon and Mallory had rejuvenated a dying town and given the population new hope. They were well suited and shared a lifetime of experiences.

Brindon deserved a woman like Mallory Peterson.

"Something's wrong," he said knowingly. "You've been prickly since the party."

"I'm tired. I just want to get home." If it could be called that.

"Do you want to skip stopping at Los Huerfanos? We can visit some other time."

"No." There wouldn't be another time. "I want to see where you grew up. Meet the Appletons." She needed to store up memories to see her through the dark days ahead.

A couple of hours later they had completed touring the grounds of Los Huerfanos Home for Boys. The headmaster encouraged them to visit the classrooms and talk to teachers and counselors, all of whom remembered Brindon from his days at the school. It was clear every adult who had ever been a part of his youth had recognized how special he was and had encouraged him to live up to his potential.

Their last stop was Ivy Cottage, one of twelve small home-like dorms housing six boys and their cottage parents. Mom and Pop Appleton reminded Dorian of Mr. and Mrs. Jack Sprat of nursery rhyme fame. The couple welcomed Brindon like a long-lost son with hugs and kisses and tears.

"Briny is our biggest success story." Mom Appleton reached up and laid her palm gently on his cheek. A short, stout woman in her late sixties, her merry eyes and plump cheeks gave her the look of perpetual good humor.

"Though it was touch-and-go there for a while," tall, spare Pop teased good-naturedly.

Brindon laughed. "The way I was headed when I got here, the fact that I didn't end up behind bars makes me a success story."

"Don't be modest," Mom scolded. "It's a sorry dog won't wag his own tail."

Brindon hugged them fiercely. "Thank you for being the mother I lost and the father I needed."

Brindon pointed the Navigator toward Dallas and set the cruise control. The sleek SUV streaked across the wide, flat plains.

"So what did you think of Los Huerfanos?" he asked.

"It's a nice place. So clean. The children seemed happy."

"The school needs a lot of improvements. A new gymnasium and sports equipment. Computers, textbooks. The headmaster told me the greenhouse was damaged in a storm last year, and they don't have the funds to replace it."

"Greenhouse?"

"The spring plant sale is the school's biggest fund-raiser. Without the greenhouse, the boys won't be able to grow the seedlings for next year's sale."

"I feel a donation coming on," she said with a smile.

"I want the boys to have what they need."

"It's a good PR opportunity," she said. "I'll call the headmaster and set up a reception. I'll need to alert the newspaper, so they can send a reporter. We can dummy up one of those huge cardboard checks for you to hand over and get one of the cute little boys to accept it on behalf of the school."

He was silent for a long time. "What…?" she asked.

"I want my contribution to be anonymous."

"That's very Brindon of you, but if you're going to give

away so much money, you might as well get something for
it. The publicity will put your name and face into the papers
in a favorable way. Millionaire orphan and all that. It's an
excellent human interest story and might even shake loose
some money from other donors.''

"That's not how it's going to be. I've instructed Malcolm
to set up a foundation account for my donations. He'll write
the check and send it to Los Huerfanos. That way no one will
know I'm involved.''

She sighed in frustration. "I don't understand. You should
use every opportunity to further your cause. I've been around
the charity world all my life. That's how it works. Be altruistic
but be smart.''

"Altruism isn't something you do for yourself, Dori.'' His
words were quiet, tight with disappointment. "It's something
you do for others. After all the time we've spent together, I
thought you would have learned that by now.''

When they arrived home, Brindon carried her bags upstairs.
He asked her to call their favorite Chinese take-out place,
while he dropped off his own luggage and took Reba out for
a walk. After ordering the food, Dorian went into her bedroom
to unpack.

Thanks to the trip to Slapdown, she knew what she had to
do. Everything pointed in the same direction. Her reception in
Brindon's hometown, the fateful arrival of Mallory Peterson.
The trip to Los Huerfanos. All signs from fate that she'd waffled back and forth between longing and desire, between
knowing and denying, long enough. She made her decision.
She would tell him tonight.

Briny sensed the coming storm and reacted the way live-
stock do before a tornado hits. Dorian's tense but polite eva-
sions made him skittish and fidgety, and he felt compelled to
move something, even if it was only a tapping toe or drum-
ming finger. She'd been remote and distant since the party last
night, and he couldn't get her to open up.

"Will you take a pill or something?'' She put down her
chopsticks in exasperation. "You're making me crazy.'' She

rose from the table and carried the take-out cartons into the kitchen.

Determined to get some answers, he followed and leaned against the counter. "You've been making me crazy all day." He grabbed her arm playfully as she walked by and pulled her close. Before his lips could find hers, she wriggled out of his grasp.

"Don't do that."

He grinned, uncertain of the game she was playing. "If you don't want me to kiss you, I have some other ideas we could try."

"Stop it. Don't say those things." With a vicious jab, she poked her leftovers down the garbage disposal and flipped the switch.

He stepped behind her and wrapped his arms around her waist, feathering gentle kisses on the soft skin at her nape. God, he longed to kiss her, hold her. Make love to her. Last night at the trailer, he'd practically had to barricade himself in his bedroom to keep from breaking down the door to her room. He'd lain in bed, tortured with the knowledge that she was so close.

It tore his heart out to think she was pulling away from him, because sometime during the long, lonely night he had made up his mind to ask her to marry him. He leaned in for another pass at her lips, but she turned her head and yanked away. "What is wrong with you?" he demanded more sharply than he intended.

"Nothing."

"Dammit! Stop lying to me and start talking." Desperation made him frantic. He was losing the war, and he didn't even know when the battle lines had been drawn. "I've been patient because I know you have a lot to work through. But I'm tired of being Mr. Nice Guy if all you're going to do is push me away. I want to know what is going on."

She washed and dried her hands, then tossed the kitchen towel onto the counter as though throwing down the gauntlet. "You really want to know, Brindon?"

"Yes!"

"Fine. I'll tell you."

"It's about time." He didn't know whether to feel relieved or worried. He thought they would become engaged tonight. How had they gotten from that happy point to this miserable one? "I thought we had an understanding. You know how I feel about you. But you've acted strangely all day." He raked his hand through his hair. "I'm confused. I don't know what you want."

"I want you to go away."

Her words struck him like a hard slap in the face. Or a punch in the gut. He felt as if he'd stepped off a roof and down was the only option. "Go where?"

"Back to Slapdown. That's where fate wants you to be. Not here. Not with me." She wheeled around and stalked into the living room. "I respectfully request to be released from our contract immediately. I can put it in writing, if you want." She opened the front door and leaned against it. "Have Malcolm handle the details. If you move out of the downstairs apartment soon, there will be no need for us to see each other or to speak again."

No need for them to speak? Briny grabbed her arm and slammed the door. Her eyes widened in surprise, and he saw the glittering flash of fear. She was afraid of him? God. How had things gone so wrong? "What the hell are you talking about, Dori?"

"Don't call me that." Her voice was angry, her words cruel. "I'm Dorian. I will never be Dori. Don't you understand?"

"No, I do not understand!" His own voice was almost as angry as hers.

"I'm not Dori, but Mallory is. Mallory is Dori."

He held her arm, afraid that if he let her go, he would lose her forever. He fought to regain control. "You're not making sense. Dammit, Dori, what is going on here," he pleaded. "You have to tell me!"

So she did.

"If you're smart, Brindon, you'll court Slapdown's new doctor and marry her as soon as you can put a ring on her finger. Start raising babies that will have a one-hundred-percent chance of inheriting good genes.''

"What?" Briny was confused by the sudden turn of events. Dorian seemed to be speaking in an unknown tongue. "What makes you think I'm interested in Mallory?"

"She's the woman you need."

"Mallory Peterson is like a little sister to me." He didn't know what else to say. "It's you I love. You, Dori."

"No! You can't love me. I don't have the capacity to change enough to make a relationship work. For a while, I thought I could. Now I know better."

"But I thought…what happened to change your mind?" He swung around in impotent frustration. "C'mon. You're gonna have to help me out here." He was losing her, and he didn't know how to get her back. "Why are you driving me away?"

She blinked away the tears that filled her eyes. "I stopped believing in fairy tales."

Chapter Thirteen

The day after Dorian told him she didn't want to see him again, a stunned Briny moved out of the downstairs apartment and back into the hotel where he'd lived when he'd first arrived in Dallas. Over the next couple of weeks, he met with Malcolm to discuss endowment of the Marion Tucker Foundation, the charitable organization he'd created and named for his mother. Based on his research, he chose the donations, grants and scholarships he deemed worthy and arranged for the foundation to distribute the funds annually.

He busied himself wrapping up financial loose ends, but could not stop thinking about Dorian. Since the night she'd sent him away, he'd gone from stunned and disbelieving to brokenhearted and resigned, but still couldn't believe she was out of his life. Maybe forever. He tried to call her at home and on her cell phone to profess his love and promise to do whatever he had to do to make her believe him.

He always got her voice mail.

Through Malcolm he learned her grandmother had returned from the Mediterranean, and Dorian was staying with her at the Burrell ranch fifty miles outside of Dallas. He was tempted to drive there and demand she see him one more time, but he knew better than to try to force Dorian to change her mind when it was so stubbornly made up.

He didn't know what else to do, so he resolved to give her time to realize her mistake and acknowledge how much she missed him. Hopefully, his plan wouldn't backfire, and he would yet have a chance to convince her of his love.

At the end of September, he returned to Slapdown to take part in ground-breaking ceremonies for the new clinic, but his heart wasn't in it. He was amazed by the boom in business in town since his last visit, but would have enjoyed the town's growth even more if Dorian had been with him to share in the excitement.

After the ceremony he met Mallory at the diner for a cup of coffee. They had to wait for a table, due to the unprecedented number of customers filling the small dining room. Two new antique shops had recently opened on Main Street, and news was getting out that Slapdown was a good place to find a bargain.

They slid into a recently vacated booth. "So when are you going to stop licking your wounds, Briny, and talk some sense into Dorian?" Mallory asked without preamble.

"She doesn't want to see me." He sighed. "She won't return my calls. She's made her feelings very clear."

"And that's okay with you?" she asked as the waitress poured coffee.

"No." He leaned back against the plastic seat and raked his fingers through his hair. "That most certainly is *not* okay with me."

"So what are you doing here drinking java with me, pal?"

Briny took a long sip of the dark diner brew. "I've never been opposed to making a fool of myself for a good cause, but this time I can't."

"Why not?" Mallory watched him as she stirred creamer into her cup.

"Does the phrase 'It takes two to tango' ring any bells with you, Doc? She told me to get lost and didn't mince any words. I may be a dumb old country boy, but I can take a hint."

Mallory dismissed his argument with an impatient wave of

her hand. "You are the most undumb man I've ever known. That's why I can't believe you're giving up so easily."

"What do you suggest I do? Kidnap her? Tie her to a chair and withhold potty breaks until she agrees to listen to reason?"

"Now you're talking."

He gave her a wry grin. "Thanks for the encouragement, but I still have my self-respect."

"Yeah, medical science hasn't quite figured out how to cure stubborn male pride. We're close to a breakthrough, though."

"I'm not being stubborn. Just realistic." He couldn't make Dorian love him. He'd tried that already. He'd done everything he could to fit into her life, into her world. If he bared his soul, offered his heart, and she rejected him, he wasn't sure he would ever get over the hurt.

She looked him over like a careful physician searching for symptoms. "You're a pigheaded fool, Briny Tucker."

He frowned. "Is that your considered medical opinion?"

She smiled. "Hey, you're my hero, remember? If you give up now, I may have to lose all respect for you. Since when have you been a quitter?"

"There's a big difference between giving up and letting go." He didn't like either course of action, but didn't think he had a choice.

"Remind me again, which one are you doing?"

He didn't answer for a long moment, then swallowed hard to force the pain out of his voice. "I'm letting her go."

"Why?" Mallory leaned across the table and patted his hand. "You two belong together. Any three-legged blind hound dog could see that."

"She doesn't want me. She was pretty clear on that point. I may not have a college degree, but I'm not stupid."

"But you're being mighty dense for a smart man. Despite the pulled-together act she puts on for the world, Dorian Burrell is a very insecure woman."

"I know. I tried to help her get past that, but—"

"It's not a matter of her getting past it, Briny. She has to leave it behind."

"I'm assuming you're going to explain there's a difference."

"So glad you asked. The first time I saw Dorian at Thorndyke I thought she was the prettiest, most sophisticated girl I'd ever met. But the more I learned about her, the I more I felt sorry for her. I heard the way the other girls talked about her, even the ones who were supposed to be her friends. Boys asked her out because of what she had, not because of who she was. She was the loneliest popular person I ever met. I tried to befriend her because I knew what it was like to always be on the outside looking in, never belonging."

"And?"

Mallory smiled sadly. "She wouldn't let me get close. I figured it was easier for her to have shallow friendships with other rich sorority girls than to risk having a real one with someone who might expect more from her."

"So what should I do? She won't answer my calls. If I try to force her to see me, she'll just crawl deeper down that hole she's dug herself into. Then I might never reach her. I can't risk pushing her to make a decision about our future. Doing that might give her more ammunition to use against me."

"True," Mallory agreed. "Forcing her hand could backfire. Is there some way you could accidentally on purpose arrange to be in the same place at the same time?" Mallory sipped her coffee. "If she was your captive audience, maybe you could talk to her, reason with her. Change her mind."

He thought about his friend's suggestion for a moment before snapping his fingers. "Yes! The Art League's Annual Autumn Gala. I know she'll be there, it's one of her pet charities. And I received an invitation."

Mallory grinned and arced her hand up over the table to smack his in a jubilant high five. "There you go, Prince Charming. Get thyself to the ball."

"I'm not going." Dorian curled up on the sofa at the ranch and pulled a chenille throw over her head. "So you can just stop talking about it."

"Of course you're going! Burrells always attend the Art

League Gala. It's tradition.'' Granny Pru yanked the cover away. "Get up off that couch, young lady. You've been moping around here, feeling sorry for yourself, ever since I got back. If I'd known you were going to lie around and pout, I would've stayed in Greece!''

"You are a mean old woman, you know that?'' Dorian's indulgent smile belied her words. She crossed the room and hugged her grandmother, whose gray hair and soft, dumpling figure concealed a no-nonsense attitude. More than one opponent had squared off with Prudence Burrell over a conference table only to discover she wasn't as sweet as she looked. "But I love you.''

"I love you, too. Now what about that boy Malcolm's been telling me about? Briny Tucker, I believe his name is. You love him, don't you?''

"Yes, but that's over. He's better off without me.''

"Land sakes, child! Are you trying to give Joan of Arc a run for her money? I'll warn you right now, you won't succeed. There has never been a martyr in the whole history of the Channing and Burrell families. We're no good at not getting what we want.''

"You don't understand.'' Dorian didn't think she could explain, or even wanted to try.

"Oh, I think I do. I haven't lived seventy-nine years with my eyes shut. I've been around the block a few times, girlie, and I recognize a broken heart when I see one.''

Granny Pru was the only person with whom Dorian could relax her guard, reveal her true feelings. She could tell her grandmother her biggest fear. "Briny is a better person than I am. He started out with nothing, and he's made a real difference in the world. I started out with everything money could buy, but I've got nothing to show for twenty-six years of living.''

Pru snorted. "That is the biggest pile of horse-doody I ever heard.''

Dorian laughed at the salty expression. Years of the good life had turned her grandmother into an elegant dowager. But under her polished exterior beat the heart of a west-Texas spit-fire. "You don't know him."

"I feel like I do. I've done some checking, and I've learned a few things about our Mr. Brindon Z. Tucker."

"Really?" Dorian didn't doubt her grandmother had the resources, but was surprised she'd gone to so much trouble. "You mean you had him investigated?"

"Yes, I did, and I'm not too proud to admit it. You're the only grandchild I have. For the record, Mr. Tucker passed inspection with flying colors. From what Malcolm tells me, and from what I learned from my other sources, he sounds just like the kind of young man I'd like to have for a grand-son."

"That has never been the problem," Dorian declared. "I've always known he was perfect. I'm the one who's lacking."

"More horse-doody! You come from good stock, Dorian Channing Burrell. Why your great-grandfather Portis Channing was a down-on-his-luck wildcatter who worked hard and dreamed big. When I was a little girl, we lived in a tar-paper shack. Ate beans and corn bread every day and were glad to have them. I've been poor and I've been rich. I have to say I like rich better, but poor can be a character-building experience."

"Is that why you cut off my funds before you went to Greece?" she asked with a wry grin. "To build my character?"

"I told Malcolm that under all that party doll fluff, you were one sharp cookie. I think my plan worked. Based on what you've told me about your activities and that software business you're thinking of getting into, you've made a good start on making your way in the world."

"I don't know how successful the company will be, Granny. Justin Green approached me about marketing computerized art programs for children. We haven't come to an agreement yet."

"You're on the right path. That spirit helped my daddy strike it rich."

"I've heard the rags-to-riches story before," she said gently.

"But you haven't seen the pictures." Granny Pru went to her room and returned with an old leather photograph album. She sat on the sofa and pulled Dorian down beside her. "I've been meaning to show you this old picture album my cousin left me when she died. That's Daddy standing in front of his first oil well. Handsome devil, wasn't he?"

"Yes." The young man in the faded photo was short and wiry with a shock of dark hair and a devil-may-care grin just like her grandmother's.

A faraway looked filled Pru's eyes as she remembered another time. "Bless his heart and rest his soul. Daddy was a good man."

Dorian recalled that Brindon had been inspired by stories of Portis Channing's generosity. She shared what he'd said with her grandmother.

"Don't you think it's queer?" the old woman asked. "That you're connected to your great-grandfather like that through your young man. Like the hand of fate was stirring things up."

At the mention of fate, a shiver raised goose bumps on Dorian's arms. "He's not my young man, Granny Pru."

"Oh, but he could be." She turned the pages of the album, naming relatives long dead but not forgotten.

Dorian was startled to see a face looking out at her that was eerily like her own. "Who's that?"

Pru smiled. "Why, that's my mama. Her name was Kathleen Kelly until she married my father and became a Channing."

"I look like her." The young woman in the photograph was dressed in the style of the 1920s. An old-fashioned cameo brooch held the scarf around her neck in place.

"I always thought so. You've never seen her picture before?"

"Not when she was so young."

"Katie Kelly came to Texas to teach in a one-room school. She was smart as a whip, always helping people. Once during a whooping cough epidemic, she went from farm to farm, nursing the sick until a doctor could arrive. More than one Texan owes his life to that little lady. You remind me of her.''

The resemblance was uncanny. Dorian's face had the same heart shape as her great-grandmother's. Her eyes had the same tilt at the corners, her lips the same fullness. Looking at the portrait was like peering into the mirror of time at the ancestor who had perhaps passed on to her the love of teaching. If only the resemblance were more than skin-deep, Dorian might yet become as loving and unselfish as her ancestor had been.

''I always thought I looked like Cassandra,'' she said. ''That I was more like her than anyone.''

Pru snorted. ''That'll be the day. If I thought for a minute you were anything like that little witch, I would disown you so fast it would make your head spin. I'm still mad at her for stealing you away from me after John died. But she was your mother, and there wasn't a whole hell of a lot I could do about it at the time.''

Dorian squeezed her grandmother's hand. ''We're together now.''

''And we're going to make up for the time we lost. I'm proud of the way you handled things while I was gone. I knew you had it in you, you just never had a chance to believe in yourself before.''

''That's what Brindon told me.''

''I'm liking this boy more all the time,'' Pru declared. ''He sounds like a keeper. Are you sure you want to throw him back?''

''I'm afraid it's too late.''

''Nonsense. You've seen both sides of life now. Most people born as high up the food chain as you were never get that chance. It's up to you to choose which life you want.''

Dorian sat with the old album in her lap and stared at the picture of her great-grandmother for long moments. A sense of adventure had brought Katie Kelly to Texas. Love for a handsome oil man had made her stay. If Dorian had half Katie's gumption, she wouldn't be afraid to love. She wouldn't let old hurt keep her from new love.

Dorian knew now she was nothing like her mother. If she

was, Brindon and her grandmother, both astute judges of character, would have given up on her by now. She began crying and couldn't stop. Tears of joy cleansed her spirit of the burden of the past.

"Girl? What's the matter with you?" Pru asked. "You're gonna be all puffy-eyed when you go to the party, if you don't stop that bawlin'."

"I'm happy. I know what I want," she sobbed into the lace-edged handkerchief her grandmother pressed into her hand.

"Praise the Lord. Do I need to ask?"

"Briny." Dorian smiled through her tears. "I want Briny."

"Then go after him." Pru held Dorian's hands in her worn and gnarled ones. "I've learned three things in this life, honey. Where there's a will, there's a way, and love conquers all."

"That's only two," she said with a choked laugh. "What's the third thing you learned, Granny?"

"There's no such thing as one size fits all."

On the night of the Art League's Annual Autumn Gala, the hotel's grand ballroom was transformed into a wonderland of exotic flowers and twinkling white lights. Quivering candles in delicate crystal cups lit each snowy, linen-draped table, and baskets and swaths of greenery festooned a buffet laden with rich sweets and mouthwatering delicacies, all prepared by the city's most skilled chefs.

Exquisitely garbed ladies floated on pastel clouds of organza and tulle and silk. Courtly gentlemen in elegant black tie led them around the dance floor as the elite of the Dallas Symphony Orchestra filled the rarefied air with old waltzes and new melodies.

So much extravagance…and all for a good cause.

Briny presented his invitation at the door and stepped across the threshold into another world. He felt at ease here now. He had learned to move comfortably from the alternate reality of high society to the grounding world of the Slapdown community. And back again.

He was content in his skin, pleased at the direction his life had taken. He'd fulfilled his promise and had successfully passed on most of his lottery winnings to better the lives of others. He wasn't broke, by any stretch of the imagination, but the weight of fifty million dollars was no longer a burden on his shoulders.

His gaze swept the room in search of Dorian. He knew she would be here. Burrells were big supporters of the Arts. He was about to intensify his search and make a circuit of the room when he spotted her on the other side of the dance floor. Looking like his favorite dream come true.

Her long satin gown was palest pink, the color of barely remembered roses. The beaded strapless bodice bared her shoulders, and the wide, full skirt floated around her on a whisper of air. She wore matching long satin gloves that clung to her arms and stretched above her elbows. A gauzy wrap, held together by an old-fashioned cameo, encircled her shoulders. Her hair was swept into a regal style, and delicate pink gems sparkled from her ears and in the dainty choker around her neck.

From her perfectly coifed head to her delicate satin slippers, Dorian was the personification of the princess who lived on the glass hill. Briny's breath caught, and he began to believe he had finally made it to the top of that magical hill. In the weeks they'd been apart, he'd forgotten how beautiful she was.

But he had not forgotten how much he loved her.

Dorian's skin tingled, and she knew Brindon had arrived. She had not been sure he would come, but she had hoped, as her hungry gaze searched the crowd for the sight of his face. She found him quickly, as he was always taller than the next tallest man in any room. Their eyes met, and his lips softened in the smile that had haunted her dreams.

She touched the cameo at her breast like a talisman. Granny Pru had given her Katie's brooch as a reminder of the woman she could be. Certainty flowed through Dorian like warm honey on a hot day, filling her with peace and contentment. Briny was the man she loved. She had almost let him go once. She would not make that mistake again.

She watched him amble toward her, his lean body resplendent in the Armani tux she had personally selected months before. He was the handsomest man at the ball. In the state of Texas. Powerful desire, too long denied, made her ache for his touch. The most wonderful man in the world belonged to her. The look in his eyes and the joy in her heart told her so.

"Pardon me, madam." Brindon bowed formally, just as Dorian had taught him. "May I have this dance?"

"Certainly." She placed her gloved hand upon his outstretched arm, and he whirled her onto the floor. Her heart hammered wildly, but it was not the dance that took her breath away. It was the man.

"May I have the next dance, as well?" His smile told her was enjoying their charade.

"Most certainly." Pure enchantment filled the places in her heart where she had stored the pain. She knew this joyful feeling would last as long as she and Briny were together.

"And the next?" he whispered, nibbling a path down the column of her neck. "And the next?" He dropped hot kisses on her shoulder. "And every dance forever until the world ends?"

"Yes." Forever. That's how long her love would last.

Lilting strains of "The Blue Danube" waltz filled the ballroom. As Dorian swirled around the room in the strong, sure arms of her very own charming prince, she knew fairy tales really could come true.

Epilogue

And it came to pass that a new prosperity was visited upon the village of Slapdown, in the western land called Texas. Though he bestowed his wealth upon others less fortunate, Briny the handsome, bighearted young pauper became the richest man of all.

For, as destiny had decreed, he ventured to the shining kingdom of Dallas, and there he met the one woman with whom he would live out his days. As lovely and lonely as any princess who ever graced the pages of a fable, Dori lived at the top of a glass hill, beyond the reach of happiness, where even dreams could not find her.

Briny vowed to free her from the dungeon of her doubts. Relentless in his quest, he climbed the glass hill. There he slew the dragons that guarded his true love's heart and carried her down from the hill forever.

On a mission of kindness, they traveled from her kingdom to his village, fulfilling his promise to Lady Luck. Riches were the gift they gave freely to others, and yet they kept the greatest treasure for themselves.

For the princess and the pauper learned an important truth on their journey from never to forever.

With Love All Things Are Possible.

And so it was that Briny and Dori lived happily ever after.

* * * * *

*If you liked TUTORING TUCKER,
be sure to check out
WHEN LIGHTNING STRIKES TWICE
from Debrah Morris in September 2003.*

In June 2003

Silhouette Books
invites you to share
a blessed event

Baby Love

She had promised to raise her sister's baby
as her own, with no interference from the baby's
insufferable father. But that was before she met
that darkly handsome, if impossible, man! He was
someone she was having a hard time ignoring.
Don't miss Joan Elliott Pickart's *Mother at Heart*.

Their passionate marriage was over,
their precious dreams in ashes.
And then a swelling in her belly made
one couple realize that one of their dreams
would yet see the light of day.
Look for Victoria Pade's *Baby My Baby*.

Available at your favorite retail outlet.

Don't miss the latest miniseries from award-winning author Marie Ferrarella:

Meet...

Sherry Campbell—ambitious newswoman who makes headlines when a handsome billionaire arrives to sweep her off her feet...and shepherd her new son into the world!
A BILLIONAIRE AND A BABY, SE#1528, available March 2003

Joanna Prescott—Nine months after her visit to the sperm bank, her old love rescues her from a burning house—then delivers her baby....
A BACHELOR AND A BABY, SD#1503, available April 2003

Chris "C.J." Jones—FBI agent, expectant mother and always on the case. When the baby comes, will her irresistible partner be by her side?
THE BABY MISSION, IM#1220, available May 2003

Lori O'Neill—A forbidden attraction blows down this pregnant Lamaze teacher's tough-woman facade and makes her consider the love of a lifetime!
BEAUTY AND THE BABY, SR#1668, available June 2003

The Mom Squad—these single mothers-to-be are ready for labor...and true love!

Where love comes alive™

SILHOUETTE *Romance*

COMING NEXT MONTH

#1672 COUNTERFEIT PRINCESS—Raye Morgan
Catching the Crown
When Crown Prince Marco Roseanova of Nabotavia discovered that
Texas beauty Shannon Harper was masquerading as his runaway fiancée,
he was furious—until he found himself falling for her. Still, regardless of
his feelings, Marco had to marry royalty. But was Shannon really an
impostor, or was there royal blood in her veins?

#1673 ONE BRIDE: BABY INCLUDED—Doreen Roberts
Impulsive, high-spirited Amy Richards stepped into George Bentley's
organized life like a whirlwind on a quiet morning—chaotic and uninvit-
ed. George didn't want romance in his orderly world, yet
after a few of this mom-to-be's fiery kisses…order be damned!

#1674 TO CATCH A SHEIK—Teresa Southwick
Desert Brides
Practical-minded Penelope Doyle didn't believe in fairy tales, and her
new boss, Sheik Rafiq Hassan, didn't believe in love. But their protests
were no guard against the smoldering glances and heart-stopping kisses
that tempted Penny to revise her thinking…and claim this prince as her
own.

#1675 YOUR MARRYING *HER?*—Angie Ray
Stop the wedding! Brad Rivers had always been Samantha Gillespie's
best friend, so he certainly wasn't going to let him marry a woman only
interested in his money! But was she ready to acknowledge the desire
she was feeling for her handsome "friend" and even—gulp!—propose
he marry *her* instead?

#1676 THE RIGHT TWIN FOR HIM—Julianna Morris
Was Patrick O'Rourke crazy? Maddie Jackson had sworn off romance
and marriage, so why, after one little kiss, did the confirmed bachelor
think she wanted to marry him? Still, beneath his I'm-not-the-marrying-
kind-of-guy attitude was a man who seemed perfect as a husband and
daddy.…

#1677 PRACTICE MAKES MR. PERFECT—
Patricia Mae White
Police Detective Brett Callahan thought he needed love lessons
to lure the woman of his dreams to the altar, so he convinced neighbor
Josie Matthews to play teacher. But none of his teachers had been as
sweet and seductive as Josie, and *none* of their lessons had evoked passion like this!

SRCNM0603